THE WARRIOR GOD

THE ARES TRIALS

ELIZA RAINE

ROSE WILSON

Editors: Christopher Mitchell, Lea Vickery

Cover: Yocla Designs

ELIZA RAINE
ROSE WILSON

BOOK ONE
— OF THE —
ARES TRIALS

THE WARRIOR GOD

For all those who feel they don't belong.
Your tribe is out there.

1

BELLA

"Bella, please, put me down."

I barely heard the words over the blood pounding in my ears. But I knew the voice.

"Bella, I'd really, really appreciate it if you could just let go of my neck."

The red mist was making my vision cloudy, obscuring the man in front of me, who was pinned to the wall by my hand across his throat.

But I knew his voice.

"Bella, please." The voice was scratchy and choked but...

"Joshua!" I cried, dropping my rigid arm immediately, the fury raging through my body dissipating as guilt swamped me. "Shit, shit, shit, I did it again, didn't I?"

Joshua slid down the magnolia-painted wall opposite me, clutching at his throat, his eyes red.

"Yeah. Yeah, you did."

"Why? Why am I like this?" I couldn't keep the bitterness from my voice as I crouched down to him, pulling him to his feet.

"That's what therapy is going to help you with, Bella," he said, blinking slowly and twisting his neck as we walked back toward his desk, and the long couch I always sat on.

"But I've been seeing you for months, and I'm no better." Anger started to rekindle in my gut, the frustration of not being able to control myself a delicious fuel for my rage. Nothing set off the rage like frustration.

"Anger management therapy is a long process. You're doing great," Joshua said, and sat down in his chair.

I slumped down on the patient couch and cocked my head at him. My skin was still fizzing from the adrenaline that always accompanied me getting mad.

"How many times will you let me attack you before you quit on me?" I whispered. I didn't actually want to know the answer. He was the only man who had ever tried to help me, and I couldn't face watching him suffer at my own hands over and over again.

"I'm tougher than I look, Bella. I'm not going anywhere."

He smiled at me, most of the strain on his face now gone, and I so badly wanted to believe him.

I knew it was wrong to have a crush on your shrink. But, in my defense, he was freaking hot. Dark hair flopped over his forehead and curled around his ears, and his hazel eyes were permanently calm and soothing, a balm to my own constant million-miles-an-hour energy. And he looked tough enough to me. My eyes flicked over his body.

Broad shoulders.

Rounded biceps.

Big red mark on his neck... I'd done that. I'd *just* done that. Guilt made me feel sick, twisting my stomach in knots. Joshua was the only person who had ever truly tried to help me.

But when the red mist descended, I was no longer Bella; mostly decent, if a little hyper, human being. I was a freaking maniac. And strong to boot. It was as though my anger made me physically more powerful, and dangerous. Rational thought abandoned me, my normal senses overtaken completely.

And the worst part was, I desired it. When I was younger, I hadn't tried to fight it. The feeling of strength and control was like a drug, and I allowed the craving for confrontation to run wild. I reveled in every fight I won, no matter if the person I kicked the shit out of deserved it or not. Every time someone underestimated me, at five foot two with my pixie-face and blonde hair, I took pleasure in smashing their preconceptions to bits. And it wasn't just their preconceptions I smashed. I smashed *everything*.

When I got too old for the cops to keep letting me out, I got more careful. But I didn't stop.

When I was busted for fighting in the underground gambling rings, they gave me a six-month sentence. When I fought with every cellmate I had, I was put in solitary confinement.

And then I got sad. Like really, really sad. Being

completely alone sucked. But in the absence of anyone to pick a fight with, I could think clearly for the first time in my life. I realized I needed to control my anger, and I needed to vent it on the right people. The people who deserved their asses booted into next week.

"Tell me more about your foster parents," Joshua said.

"But what if it triggers me again?"

"We need to work through your problems. I accept the risk that comes with that," he replied, gently.

I shook my head.

"No. No, I don't think we should carry on. I've already hurt you once today."

"You're not a bad person, Bella. The anger in you is chemical, it's not part of your soul. Remember that."

I said nothing. Because he was wrong. My issue wasn't a chemical imbalance. It was more than that, I was sure. I'd known something was wrong with me my whole life.

Joshua sighed. "Will you join us for the group session today?"

I nodded. I hated group therapy. Everyone there pissed me off. But Joshua insisted it was good for me, and I felt bad about what I'd done to his neck.

"Sure," I said.

"Good. Are you sure you don't want to carry on now?"

"I'm sure," I told him. Like hell did I want to keep talking about being abandoned by my asshole parents, and then being passed between money-grabbing, child-hating families for the next ten years. "I'll go for a quick run round the block, burn off some energy 'til group starts."

"Good idea," he smiled. "See you in twenty minutes."

~

"You're a decent human, you're a decent human," I chanted to myself as I jogged down Fleet Street, avoiding tourists and biting back impatient comments. God, but those morons moved slowly.

Maybe I should relocate. London was filled to the brim with angry energy. It couldn't be helping me calm down.

But I couldn't leave London. Not because I had family there or anything. Hell, I didn't even have any friends, let alone family. No, the reason I couldn't leave London was the theaters.

Since I'd moved to England from New Jersey ten years ago, I'd saved every spare bit of cash I could scrabble together from the menial, shitty jobs I could never hold on to and my bouts in the underground fights, to spend on the theater. I didn't have the patience for books, and I could barely sit still through an entire movie, but there was something completely mesmerizing about the theater to me. I attributed every moral fiber in my being to what I had learned through plays and musicals. Empathy seemed to pour into me from nowhere when I watched the fictional stories play out so vividly before me, the actors giving it everything they had and every second sucking me in further.

No, I couldn't leave London. Although since losing my last shitty job I couldn't actually afford the theater any more. But at least I'd learned a valuable lesson; I did not have the right temperament to be a bartender in a city. Drunken assholes were a big fucking trigger for my temper. I sucked in air as I jogged faster.

I'd find another job. Soon. I had to, or me and my stick-up-her-ass cat would end up hungry and homeless.

"You're a decent human," I repeated through clenched teeth, flipping my middle finger at a cyclist who was swerving around me on the wrong side of the road and swallowing back the desire to yell something obscene at him.

When I got back to Joshua's building I headed straight for the washroom and changed my t-shirt. I let my hair out of its knot on top of my head and tried to make it look somewhat attractive, then gave up, glaring at my reflection instead.

Why the hell would a man who I regularly attacked and knew how much of a freak I was, be attracted to me?

I blew out a sigh. At least he *knew* I was a freak. Unlike all the other poor bastards I'd dated. The first they'd known of it was when something innocuous triggered the mist and I went freaking crazy on their ass. Me and dating did not go well together.

But Joshua... There was something in his eyes when he looked at me, I was sure of it. Something deeper than just professional patience. He cared about me.

"Yeah, keep telling yourself that, freakface," I muttered at my reflection. But that was fear talking. Fear manifesting as shit-talking and aggression. He had taught me that, in our sessions.

I was scared he would turn me down, and then I wouldn't be able to face him again. I would lose him, and his help.

But I couldn't stop imagining how much better my life would be if he *did* like me. Imagining having someone to share each day, and night, with. Imagining him kissing me...

I stood straighter as I made my decision. I was going to tell him how I felt.

If he wasn't interested then he wouldn't be a dick about it, that wasn't his way. I would just go home with a red face, eat my bodyweight in ice cream and then spend a few hours with my punch-bag. Maybe avoid him for a week.

But if he said yes... Those soft eyes, that gentle voice, those expressive hands.

The best-case scenario outweighed the worst-case. I was going to do it.

I was early, so there was nobody else around as I pushed the double doors to the lecture room open. My heart hammered in my chest as I stepped into the room. I was really going to do it. I was going to tell him how I felt. Maybe not that I was in love with him, I didn't want to scare the shit out of him. But definitely that I was into him.

Joshua was a part-time university psychology lecturer, part-time anger management shrink. The university let him use his office for one-on-one sessions, and one of their larger lecture rooms for group. I'd never made it to university. Surprise, surprise.

Sadly, Joshua's building wasn't one of the many beautiful old university structures that dotted London and looked like something out of a fairytale. It was a concrete monstrosity built in the seventies, and the lecture room looked like any other boring office, just a bit bigger, with lots of cheap plastic chairs.

I stumbled as I reached the ring of seats set out for us crazies in the middle of the room.

Someone was lying on the floor, in the center of the circle of chairs.

Joshua.

"Joshua?" I ran forward, dropping to my knees beside him, about to turn him onto his back when I froze. *Blood.* There was blood, pooling beneath him. I watched in dazed slow-motion as the surreal-looking red liquid spread, approaching my knees. Logic seeped through my shock. If the blood was spreading now... this must have just happened.

I leaped to my feet, my fists raised, my muscles swelling as instinct took over.

"Where are you?" I roared at the unknown threat. "Show yourself!"

The air in front of me shimmered, and then there was a blinding white flash. My hands moved to cover my eyes instinctively, and I could feel the anger building inside me.

I was ready to fight.

I dropped my arms and blinked rapidly, clearing my eyes.

And gaped.

A man was standing on the other side of Joshua. And he looked like no man I'd ever seen.

He was seven feet tall at least, and was wearing gleaming golden armor like a freaking Roman soldier. His face was covered by a massive shining helmet with a red plume, and his arms and legs were made of muscle, thick ropes of it wrapping around his limbs like Arnold fucking Schwarzenegger.

He reached out with his sandaled foot and poked at Joshua.

"What the fuck are you doing?" I yelled, darting toward him. "Why have you done this?"

The eyes in the helmet snapped to mine.

"You are more interested in challenging me than saving him? That confirms it. You are the right one," the man said, his voice deep and abrupt. His words took me aback, and I realized he was right. I needed to help Joshua.

I shoved my hand in my jeans back pocket, pulling out my cellphone and fumbling to unlock it.

"Stay right there! I don't know why you've done this, but I'm calling the police!"

The man ignored me, flipping Joshua over with his

foot, and there was an awful squelching noise. Blood soaked the front of his shirt, and his eyes were glassy and staring. I froze, senses swimming.

"Is he dead?" Please, please, please don't let him be dead, I prayed, the backs of my eyes burning.

"Yes. He is dead."

I felt a wave of dizziness wash over me, my stomach flipping.

"No, no, he can't be." I dropped to my knees again, feeling for a pulse in his neck.

There was nothing.

"His human body is dead. The police will think you did this," said the man simply.

"What?"

"You are here, alone with the body. And human police are fools."

"*Human* police? Who the hell are you?"

I stared up at the armored giant, my head swirling, red seeping into my vision. This couldn't be happening.

"I am Ares, God of War."

"Ares? The fucking Greek god?"

"Yes. Stop saying fuck. It is unladylike."

"Unladylike?" I realized I was yelling as I got unsteadily to my feet. "Why did you kill him?"

"Stupid girl. I did not kill him. And only his human body is dead. His soul has been stolen, taken to Olympus."

I felt myself sway slightly, then a surge of adrenaline shot through my veins, steadying me.

"You need to start talking sense, right now," I hissed.

The huge man glared at me a few seconds, then sighed.

"I am Ares, the God of War. And you are Enyo, Goddess of War. I did not kill him, but I am here to kill you."

2

BELLA

A normal person, on being told that an armored giant was there to kill them, would run a freaking mile, as fast as possible.

But true to form, my instincts kept me slap-bang where I was, fists raised, red mist taking over.

"Just try it, armor-boy," I snarled. All sensible thoughts, the ones about Joshua and the police and how the hell this guy had appeared out of nowhere, or what he'd just said about me being a damned *goddess*, were relegated to the back of my mind, to make space for the swell of anger and violence that was spreading through me.

He may be bigger than me, but I was stronger than I looked. *A lot stronger.* And I didn't always fight fair.

Slowly, he drew a gleaming sword from a sheath at his side. It was almost as long as I was, and my aggression wavered just a tiny bit. I'd never fought anyone with a sword before.

First time for everything.

I dropped my stance, bending my knees, ready.

"Are you not going to run away?" he asked me, his voice still calm.

"No, I'm not, you fucking maniac. I'm going to keep you here until the police arrive."

"At which point I would vanish, and you would be arrested," he said.

"We'll see about that," I spat, though part of me knew he was right. But that part of me had no control whatsoever over the rest of my body.

My legs were almost vibrating with pent-up energy, my vision now completely red.

The giant lifted his sword.

A flash of green light filled the room, and I saw a new figure directly in front of me, small and... furry. Shock rocked through me as I blinked, and the giant gave a bark of anger.

"Zeeva?" I stammered.

My cat was sitting between me and the giant.

My short-haired, uptight, tuna-eating Siamese cat. Just sitting there, like it was totally normal.

"What in the name of sweet fuck is going on?" I breathed, blinking hard.

The man I was secretly in love with being murdered by an armored giant was something my violence-addled brain could react to. But my fucking cat appearing out of thin air at the scene of the crime?

Nope. Too much.

My fists dropped to my sides in bewilderment as Zeeva turned to me, her amber eyes as disdainful and aloof as they always were.

"Bella, you are a fool," a cool woman's voice sounded in my head. *"Next time you are faced with fighting a god, run."*

I opened my mouth to speak but nothing came out.

I'd lost it. I'd actually lost it. Maybe none of this was happening, and Joshua was fine. Maybe he'd visit me in the lunatic asylum.

Maybe not.

Zeeva began glowing turquoise, and my jaw hung even lower as she began to grow, not stopping until she was the size of a freaking lion. But her head was still that of a Siamese cat, her pointed ears and almond shaped eyes just larger.

"Ares, you may not just take her power from her by killing her. You must earn it."

The woman's voice issued from the cat loudly, and I felt my knees wobble.

"You do not understand the seriousness of the situation!" barked Ares.

"I understand perfectly. Hera has informed me. Zeus attacked you and you lost your power. But you may not take Enyo's without first earning it."

I felt my mouth opening and closing like a freaking goldfish as I stared between them.

The giant glared at my huge cat, fury in his eyes, then slammed his sword back into its sheath.

"Fine. We go to Olympus then," he snapped, and the world flashed white around me.

When the light cleared from my eyes for the second time in five minutes, I was absolutely positive I had gone mad.

I was standing on a white marble floor, and instead of walls either side of me, there were giant flames. And they weren't orange, like normal fire, they were multi-colored – purple and green and red, dancing together mesmerizingly. A cough drew my attention, and my dumbstruck gaze shifted to what was in front of me.

Thrones. Two thrones, with people sitting on them. Well, one person. A beautiful young woman with white hair, a green dress, and a crown made of roses with gold thorns. The other throne, the one apparently made out of freaking skulls, was occupied by a figure made completely of smoke.

"Ares, what have you done now?" a hissing male voice asked, coming from the smoke person.

"How did you flash without your power?" added the woman, then gave me a small smile as she ran her eyes over me. "Don't panic, it's all real, and you'll get used to it," she said quickly to me.

I opened my mouth wider to answer, but nothing but a small squeak came out. I closed it again. The red mist had abandoned me for the first time in my life and my brain had just frozen, along with my body. What-ever was happening simply couldn't be happening.

"This is Enyo," the armored giant grunted, pointing at me. "The power of war was split between us, and then she was... lost to the mortal world." I blinked at him. "When I am with her, I can access that power, as it is the same as mine." He ground the words out like they were being forced from his lips.

What the hell was going on?

"The power was split between you?" asked the woman, and Ares nodded.

"Yes, Queen Persephone." Persephone? Did that make the smoke guy on the skull throne Hades?

This was fucking crazy. I mean, I love a bit of Greek mythology as much as the next girl, but this couldn't be real.

"Why was the power split? Are you two related?"

A weird spluttering sound bubbled from my mouth as I looked in horror between them, the absurdity of the idea jolting my reactions back to life. I had no family.

"For the love of sweet fuck, do not tell me that we are related," I breathed. He glared at me through the eye slits in his helmet, and I noticed the color of his eyes without meaning to. They were the hue of choco-late, rich and dark and... lost.

"We are not related. We could not be further from each other in lineage. I am descended from..." he paused and took a deep breath. "I am descended from Zeus. She is descended from an unknown Titan."

"I'm what now?" I asked, my eyebrows so high they were making my face hurt. Confusion was making my head swim, and the shot of adrenaline that usually came with my anger and made me rock-steady before a fight just wasn't coming.

Just treat it as a play, I told myself. *They're actors. Don't freak out.* "You're talking about Zeus and Titans. And my cat can speak." I put my hands on my hips, and closed my eyes as I sucked in air, dizziness pricking dangerously at me. "My only friend just got killed, and I'm fairly sure armor-boy did it. Someone, please tell me what the hell is going on."

When I opened my eyes Persephone was glaring at Ares, a faint green glow around her.

"Did you kill a mortal?" She asked him, her voice laced with steel.

"No! He was already dead. And besides, he wasn't mortal. There was guardian magic around him. Only his human body was destroyed."

The word 'destroyed' used to describe Joshua made me feel sick, but I clung to his words, trying to make sense of them.

"If he's not dead, where is he? What the fuck is going on?" I said, louder this time. Frustration was whipping through me like a storm, battering at my disbelief.

"Sorry, Enyo," Persephone said, with a small nod.

"Bella," I snapped, correcting her automatically, then regretting interrupting her. "My name is Bella," I mumbled.

"OK. Bella. Here's the short version. I, like you, once lived in the mortal world without knowing about Olympus. This is a world run by gods, filled with immortals and magic and creatures we knew as myth and legend. Zeus, the King of the Gods, recently made a very big mistake, and now my husband, Hades, rules in his place, in turn with Poseidon."

I stared at her until she carried on.

"Zeus is missing now, but before he left he fought with Ares, and took his power away. Zeus is extremely strong, and something like that can't be reversed."

"Yes, it can. If I kill her I can take her power," interrupted Ares. I threw him my best 'shut the hell up' look and turned back to Persephone.

"What happened to Joshua?" I had a hundred other questions, but that one was the most important.

Persephone frowned, and looked at the smoky form next to her. When he spoke again, the hissing sound was gone from his voice.

"This is not the first report I've heard of guardians being taken from the mortal realm," he said.

"Guardians?"

"There are many of them, all making sure that people like you - with power that does not belong in the mortal realm - don't cause, or attract, any trouble."

Indignation spiked in me, but faded fast. I both caused and attracted trouble all the time. There was little point in denying that.

"So Joshua knew about all this?" I waved my hands around the room, and the flames either side of me leaped and danced in response.

"Yes. He will have known you had power and would have been trying to help you manage it. I doubt he knew who you truly were. Just that you were of Olympus."

Disappointment speared my gut. Along with a dull sense of betrayal.

"And my cat?"

"I don't know," answered Persephone, looking curiously at Zeeva. I looked down at her too, normal-sized now and sitting a foot away from me. As usual, she didn't deign to look back at me.

"I was assigned to watch over Enyo a long time ago," the woman's voice from earlier said.

"By who?" asked Persephone, before I could ask the same thing.

"Hera," she answered, and Persephone smiled.

"Hera is a kind goddess and a fair ruler," she said to Zeeva, and the traitorous freaking cat actually nodded her head at the Queen.

"So..." I rubbed my hands across my face. "Just to confirm, you're saying me and my cat have magic powers and are from a secret Greek mythology world?"

"You have the power of war. It is mostly anger, strength and violent tendencies," said Ares gruffly.

Well, I mean, that would explain a lot. Like, a hell of a lot. Maybe this wasn't so cream-cracker crazy after all.

"And Joshua and other... *Guardians* have gone missing?"

"We do not have time for this!" Ares snapped, stamping his foot on the marble. I didn't flinch, straightening my own spine instead as a response. Other people's rage triggered my own, and I clung to the solidifying feeling, the sharpening of my focus. "I need my power back, before my realm discovers what has happened and rebels against me!" Ares shouted.

"We need to find Joshua!" I protested, looking at him. "Fuck your stupid powers; a man has been kidnapped!" A vision of Joshua's lifeless face flashed through my mind, and I clamped my jaw shut, trying to hold on to my fragile focus.

I needed to concentrate on one thing at a time, and that had to be finding Joshua. He may have lied to me about who or what he really was, and who or what I was for that matter, but he *had* been helping me. And now I was the only person that knew what had happened to him. I was all he had.

Understanding all this other madness would have to wait; I needed to make sure he was safe first.

"My powers are significantly more important than the disappearance of some minor guardian," said Ares. My fists clenched, but Hades spoke, and we both turned to him.

"Ares, you may not kill Enyo for her power. I forbid it."

The god of war snarled, and I failed to stop myself giving him a sarcastic smile and a middle finger flip. He bared his teeth at me.

"There is another way you can gain your power back, as we have already discussed. Oceanus is the only being stronger than Zeus. Ask him for help."

"Hades, I am not a puppet and I will not ask a Titan for help!" Ares said loudly. His enormous body was practically bulging out of his armor as his muscles tensed. I recognized the signs of trying to contain a fierce temper.

"Then you are destined to be powerless forever,"

shrugged the smoke figure. "Unless she agrees to share her power with you voluntarily."

"Why would I help him?" I exclaimed. "He's an asshole! For all I know, he kidnapped Joshua himself!"

"He is not guilty of that crime," said Hades.

"Being an asshole, or kidnapping my friend?" I snapped back.

"The kidnapping," Hades said after a pause, in which I was sure I heard a chuckle. "A number of demons escaped the Underworld in the chaos of Zeus' fleeing. I have reason to believe that one of these demons is responsible, and I have heard they are seeking refuge in Ares' realm."

"That is not my problem," barked Ares.

"As ruler of Olympus, I am making it your problem. I want you to find this escaped demon and the stolen Guardians. I have no authority in your lawless land. It must be you."

"If I return to my realm, I will be overthrown without my power!"

"Then you and Bella must work together."

"No. I want no part of this," said Ares.

"It is my command as your King, Ares," said Hades, and the slither was back in his voice. An icy fear began to creep over me, and an impulse to hide clawed up my throat. The feeling was alien to me, and panic started to grip my chest, my breath coming fast.

"She's still human, my love," said Persephone gently, and the fear lessened quickly. She turned back to us and spoke clearly. "Ares, you must do as your king commands. Bella, if you want to find your friend, the assistance of Ares, one of the twelve rulers of Olympus, will be invaluable. You would be foolish to turn down help such as that."

The finality, and sense, of her words were impossible to ignore, despite every part of me railing against the idea of working with this giant idiot. He was as likely to kill me as help me.

But I had no choice.

"I have to find Joshua," I said. "I'm the only person in his life who knows he's gone missing. I'm all he has."

Persephone's eyes softened, and she laid her hand on the arm of the smoky form beside her. Their love was almost tangible, it rolled from them like physical power. I felt a little bolt of jealousy, and turned it fast into resolve. If I found Joshua and kicked the ass out of whoever had taken him, maybe I could have some of that for myself.

"Then it is settled. There will be a small ceremony to see you both on your quest," said Hades, then there was a bright flash and he disappeared.

"Ceremony? What? We have to find Joshua! We don't know why he was taken, we have to find him now, before he's..." I trailed off, not wanting to finish the sentence. I couldn't bring myself to say 'dead', not after seeing his body on the floor in a pool of blood.

The weirdness of the whole situation rocked through me again, making me shiver, and I forced it down. *Focus on one thing at a time, Bella. Laser-focus.*

"All in good time, Bella. We must wait for Hades. In the meantime, I think you need a bit of background on your new surroundings," said Persephone.

"What I need is a fucking big drink," I answered hotly, then instantly felt guilty. She was trying to help me. To my surprise, she grinned at me.

"When I first got here, a big drink was just what I needed too."

3

BELLA

Persephone flashed us to a huge room with enormous arched windows all along one side revealing a green forest beyond. I hadn't expect Ares to accompany us and I glared at him.

"Why are you here?" I asked, as Persephone made her way to a long counter. The center of the room was dominated by a long, grand dining table.

"I can't use my power without you," he answered, sounding like he'd rather be anywhere in the world than by my side.

"Well I need some time alone. To find out what the hell is going on, and to organize myself," I said firmly. It was true. But mostly I just wanted him gone.

"You swear too much," he said, after a pause. I heard Persephone laugh as I felt myself scowl.

"I'll swear as much as I fucking like," I snapped.

"You called me an asshole. That is rude."

"You were planning to kill me! I'd say that's more rude than calling someone who is clearly an asshole an asshole!" Anger was pumping through me and his eyes narrowed.

"Stop calling me an asshole," he snarled.

"Alright. How's fuckwit?" A favorite insult in London. "Or maybe shitface?"

He took a step toward me and I raised my fists, but Persephone's level voice cut across us.

"Here's that drink you wanted, Bella." I turned to her, reluctant to take my eyes from the armored giant. "Ares, we need some girl-time," she said, and flicked her hand. I heard Ares shout as light flashed, then he was gone.

I let out a sigh of relief.

"Thank god for that. He's freaking crazy."

"He's not the worst of them," she smiled at me.

"Really?" I took the drink she offered me, and she held up her own in her other hand.

"Really. I know how you're feeling. But trust me when I tell you, accepting it quickly is easier than pretending none of it is true."

I gulped down half of my drink, and a pleasant warmth flooded from my throat down my chest.

"Actually, I've always known something was wrong with my life. To be honest, this sort of makes sense." Persephone chuckled, and sipped from her own glass.

"I wish I'd found it that easy."

The truth was, it felt more right than it should have. Perhaps the need to find Joshua wasn't the only thing keeping a total meltdown at bay. I actually felt like I'd been waiting for someone to come and drop a shit-storm like this on my head all my life. Admittedly,

'Bella, you've got magic war power' was not the form I had expected the shitstorm to take, but it made sense right down to my core. The more I thought about me being from somewhere that wasn't the shitty world I lived in, where I simply didn't belong, the more something pleasant and right tingled through my body. It was the same part of me that fueled my anger and strength. The part of me I'd spent my life trying and failing to understand and control.

It was almost a relief.

Plus, it might explain why my parents abandoned me.

"Erm, thank you, and Hades, for not letting Ares kill me," I said to Persephone.

"You're welcome. Bella, you should talk to your cat. Hera wouldn't have assigned someone to watch over you personally unless you were important."

"Ares said I was the Goddess of War. Is that important?"

"I don't know. There *isn't* a Goddess of War," she said slowly. "I can't tell you anything about your past, but I can tell you a little about Olympus. All of the Olympian gods here rule their own realms. There were twelve, until Hades created a new one, and gave it to Oceanus, who is a Titan. That's a big deal because the Olympians and the Titans fought a war a long time ago, and they still don't really get on. Zeus hates Titans."

"Didn't Ares say I'm descended from a Titan?" I felt guilty for drinking and asking questions about myself whilst Joshua was out there somewhere, but I couldn't see what else I could do. I may as well use the time to learn something useful.

"Yes. Many citizens of Olympus are. But it's only recently that they began being accepted in society."

"Great. I'm a freak here too," I muttered, and drained the rest of my glass. Persephone laughed.

"You won't be saying that when you see some of the creatures who live here. You'd have to be pretty special to stand out in Olympus. We're currently in Hades' realm, the Underworld, also known as Virgo. The realms are all star signs in the mortal world. Ares' realm is, unsurprisingly, Aries."

"Who owns Taurus?" I asked, before I could stop myself. That was my star sign.

"Dionysus, god of wine. And it's an awesome place. Unlike Ares' realm, which is home to the most violent tribes in Olympus. Everyone there is ruthless, well-trained and power hungry. It's dangerous enough that it's rarely visited by anyone."

"Right," I said, ripples of trepidation making their way through my body. Was it wrong that Aries sounded a little bit cool to me? "And that's where I'm from?"

"I don't know. Talk to Zeeva. She can probably help you more than I can. I'm only just learning a lot of this now. I've still not visited all of the other forbidden realms myself."

"There are forbidden realms?"

"Yes. Aphrodite, Artemis, Hephaestus, and Hades all have an 'invite-only' policy on their worlds."

"Have you been to Aries?" I asked.

"Yes. I've visited the Queen of the Amazons, in the south," Persephone nodded.

"Queen of the Amazons?"

"Yes. The queen is Ares' daughter."

"Huh. He doesn't look the dad type," I said slowly.

"Parentage is a bit weird with gods. My mother is a god, but I've never met her. They kind of drop kids and bolt."

"Doesn't sound that weird," I muttered, aware of my bitter tone. Persephone gave me an understanding smile.

"There's no familial attachment here. Gods are immortal, and love and family are nothing like what we grew up with."

"You and Hades seem pretty tight," I said.

"We are bonded," she beamed, and I squashed down another stab of jealousy. "Hera, goddess of marriage, linked us with magic. It is as unbreakable as immortality itself."

"Sounds like a big commitment," I said, and set my glass down on the long table. Persephone picked it up, and carried it back to the counter.

"The biggest," she replied, as she filled it back up with amber liquid. "Speaking of Hera, I will leave you and Zeeva to talk until Hades returns."

"But what about Joshua? The longer we don't know where he is, the more chance there is that something awful will happen to him."

"Bella, if whoever has taken him wanted to kill him, they would have done so when they killed his human body. Hades says that Guardians have strong magic, I'm sure your friend is fine."

I scowled at her, but said nothing, sipping at my drink instead. If her precious Hades had been kidnapped, I bet she wouldn't be so damned calm. But she was being kind to me, and I had no way of achieving anything without the help of these people.

I had a lot of questions that needed answers, that was for sure, but the priority was saving Joshua. I was the only person who knew he was in trouble. Only after he was safe, would I be able to work out what all this meant for me.

Persephone left me with my topped-up glass of whatever-it-was, and I fell into one of the many chairs. A small flash of teal light shone from somewhere on the floor and I frowned.

"Hello, Enyo," said a woman's voice in my head, and I jumped in surprise so hard that liquid sloshed from my glass.

"Get the fuck out of my head!"

"Do not swear at me. I have watched you for longer than you can possibly imagine, and I know your bluff means nothing." Zeeva jumped up onto the table in front of me and sat slowly. Gracefully. I narrowed my eyes at her.

"Why have you never spoken to me before? And how are you talking in my head? And why are you even here?"

"I had no reason to speak to you before now. I am a creature of magic with the capacity for mental communication, it is common in Olympus. Why I'm here is not your business."

"Not my business? Are you joking? Of course it's my business!"

The cat let out a long mental sigh and flicked her tail. My head swam. Zeeva was definitely the part of this my brain was struggling the most with. I mean, she was hardly an affectionate house pet, but that had been part of why I liked her. She had as much of an attitude problem as I did. If I'd known she was a freaking... Wait, what *was* she?

"What kind of 'creature of magic' are you?" I asked her.

"I am a sphinx hybrid," she answered, after a pause.

"Sphinx? Don't they ask riddles?"

"Yes. If I were to ask you a riddle that you couldn't answer, I would then have to kill you, so please don't ask for one," she said dryly. My mouth fell open.

"You could kill me?"

"Of course."

"Why are you here? I don't understand." I scrubbed my hands across my face for what felt like the twentieth time.

"Drink more nectar. It will help you think more clearly," she instructed. I looked down at my glass. I was drinking nectar?

"Please tell me why you are here. Or at least that you can help me save Joshua," I asked, changing my tone to pleading as I picked up the glass. Aggression wasn't going to work with her, clearly.

"I was assigned to watch you by Hera. She has a special interest in you. The power of war was split between you and Ares, as he said. Yours has been suppressed by such a long period in the mortal realm, but it will awaken the longer you are here. And Ares will be able to access it."

"Two questions," I said, holding up my hand to stop her. "One, how long have I been in the mortal realm? I'm twenty-nine and I don't remember being a baby, so I'm guessing it was around then?"

Zeeva blinked at me. *"What is question two?"* she asked.

"How does this power-sharing thing work? If Ares is using my power, can I use it at the same time? Or is it like a take-it-in-turns scenario? Because Ares doesn't strike me as the type of guy to share his toys."

"I have no idea. I didn't believe he would ever come for you, or that you would return to Olympus."

"Right. Great." That's helpful. *Not.* "So... Question one? How long have I been away?"

"That is inconsequential."

Anger spiked in my veins. "If you won't answer my questions and you don't know how any of this works, what exactly can you help me with?" I asked her sharply.

"I am not here to help you. I am here to report back to my Queen on your activities."

"You're a spy?"

A gleam of something dangerous flashed across her

amber eyes. *"Call me whatever you wish, Enyo, I will be keeping my eye you until this is resolved."*

"My name's Bella, not Enyo," I snapped, swigging angrily at my nectar.

"Which is short for Bellona, the Roman name for the goddess of war, which is derived from the word 'bellum', the Latin word for warfare."

I gaped at the cat. "How can you possibly know what my name is short for? I never even met the people who named me."

"I have been with you for a long time."

"No, I bought you eight years ago. You couldn't possibly have known my parents. Could you?" I couldn't keep the hope from my voice, and I could swear the look in the cat's eyes softened.

"There is too much for your mostly mortal brain to process right now. When you have proven to me that you can handle it, I will tell you more," Zeeva said eventually. I scowled, opening my mouth to protest, but the dangerous gleam flickered back instantly, and her body glowed teal. *"Do not push me, Enyo, or I will tell you nothing."*

I clamped my mouth shut, clinging to the resolve I had earlier. I couldn't do anything in Olympus without help. If the cat knew things I wanted to know, I couldn't force her to tell me. I'd have to win her trust.

"Fine. But can you please call me Bella?" I said.

"Very well."

"What's your real name?" I asked her.

"Zeeva."

"But... that's what I named you. You must have had a name before that."

"I did. Zeeva."

"Wait, did you get inside my head and choose your own name?" I asked, gaping.

"That's enough conversation for one day," she said, and jumped down off the table. *"Hades is back."*

"Wait! That's not fair!"

There was a little flash of teal light, and my traitorous magic cat was gone.

4

BELLA

I didn't know how she knew, but Zeeva was right about Hades. Before I'd even finished the rest of my nectar, Hades, Ares, and Persephone appeared at the other end of the room.

Ares' presence instantly set my nerves on edge, my anger responding to his instinctively. I stood up.

"The Olympians and a few guests are on their way. You will be leaving within a few hours," Hades said, his smoke figure turning to face me.

"They love a bit of drama here, Bella. You'll get used to it," Persephone added.

And she wasn't kidding.

After a few minutes of nervous waiting, no less than thirty people appeared out of nowhere, and boy did they test my not-freaking-out abilities. A long dais lined with thrones had appeared with them at the end of the room, and eight of the grand seats were occupied. I ran my eyes fast along the row of what I was sure were the other Olympians, my suspicions confirmed when everyone else in the room bowed low to them. I quickly did the same, desperate to take in everything around me and not knowing where to start.

Start with the gods, I decided, as I straightened. They emanated power, and my knowledge of Greek mythology was decent enough to give a pretty good guess at who they all were. Poseidon was in the middle, and the most obvious. He was wearing a toga the color of the ocean, had black hair streaked with grey, and was holding a trident. The hot-older-guy look was seriously working for him. Next to him was a severe but beautiful-looking woman with blonde hair wrapped around her head like a crown and a white toga. The owl on her shoulder gave her away as Athena. On Poseidon's other side was the most stunning woman I'd ever seen. Her skin was the color of mocha and her hair was candy pink, rolling over her shoulders and sheer blue dress in waves. She had to be Aphrodite. I was squarely into guys, but just looking at her made my insides feel weird. Next to her was a hunchback guy with a leather apron on, who must have been her husband Hephaestus. On his right was a young girl with an enormous bow and tube of arrows and gleaming armor, and next to her a ridiculously pretty guy in matching armor. He was wearing a beaming smile. The twins, Artemis and Apollo. Back at the other end of the row was a guy in tight leather trousers and an open denim shirt, with long wavy black hair and a lazy grin. Next to him was a man with a red beard and scruffy red hair, wearing a plain black toga that only made the fluttering silver wings on his sandals stand out more. Dionysus and Hermes.

I had already been told that Zeus was missing, but I was disappointed not to see Hera. I wanted to know why she'd sent a miserable freaking cat to keep an eye on me for years.

"So. You're the reason Ares has been so secretive," said a voice behind me, and I spun around.

A woman with boobs so big they barely fit in the corseted red dress she was wearing was giving me a narrow-eyed look, a half-smile on her handsome face. "Interesting."

"Who are you?" I asked. I didn't have the patience or inclination to be polite to her if that's how she was going to start a conversation. A more genuine smile tipped her lips up, and she brushed a strand of black hair out of her face.

"I'm his sister, Eris. Who are you?"

"Bella."

"Bella," she repeated, and a sudden urge to do something completely outrageous, like take all my clothes off, gripped me. Eris gave a tinkling laugh. "Oh, you're a susceptible one," she grinned, her eyes sparkling with either mischief or malice, I couldn't tell. "I like you."

"Erm," I said, concentrating hard on stopping my hands from undoing the snap on my jeans. "Are you doing this?"

"Doing what?" she purred innocently, then a cackling laugh bubbled from her lips. "Sorry, it's too easy,

I'll stop," she said, and the feeling vanished. I scowled at her.

"Don't fucking do that again."

"But I'm the Goddess of Chaos and Discord, I can't help myself," she pouted. "What are you a goddess of? I hope it's something fun. I can tell you have power, and you don't come across very innocent."

"Erm, war, apparently," I said, my eyes widening as I saw *something* walk behind her. "What in the name of sweet fuck is that?" I breathed. Eris ignored the question, her eyes lighting up.

"War? You're the goddess of war?"

"So I'm told. Seriously, what *is* that?" I pointed at the creature who had now stopped loping across the room and was talking to a woman with a lopsided face and leathery wings. Eris turned and waved her hand dismissively.

"That's a griffin talking to a harpy. Who told you that you were the Goddess of War?"

"Ares did. What the hell is a griffin?" I'd heard of a harpy, but not a griffin. He had a beak for a nose, huge torn wings, and legs like the back legs of a lion.

"Lion-eagle cross. Let me get this right. Ares told you that you were the Goddess of War? This is too good."

She was beaming as I dragged my attention from the griffin back to her face.

"Why?"

"Oh, I'm sure you'll find out soon enough. Come, let me show you some more beasties of Olympus. That over there is a minotaur, he's Hades' captain of the guard in fact, and that is a centaur. They're reclusive creatures, never leave that stuck-up bore Artemis' realm if they can help it."

My mouth fell open as I stared at the centaur. She was freaking magnificent. The bottom half of her body was that of a white mare, and rising from the horse's chest was the torso of a warrior woman. Gleaming silver armor and a belt hung with axes and war hammers wrapped around her body, and white hair the color of the horse's coat was pushed back from her stern face with a silver band.

Strength and fearlessness and battle-bravery stirred inside me as I stared at her.

"She's ready for war," I breathed, without even realizing I was speaking aloud.

"Well, you would know," said Eris. "Being Goddess of War, and all that." She said the words with barely-contained delight, and suspicion roused me from my fascination with the centaur.

"Why are you so excited about this?"

"Because my brother can be a complete fucking asshole, and you might just provide me with some entertainment."

"Well, we agree on that at least. Your brother is an asshole. He wanted to kill me."

"Wanted? I would amend that to 'wants', sweetie. Present tense. I highly doubt he's stopped wanting to kill you; Ares wants to kill most things."

"Great. Any tips on *not* being killed by him?"

"Nope. But I look forward to seeing if you survive."

"Thanks," I said, loading my voice with sarcasm.

"You're welcome," she smiled, and an urge to run over and slap the serious centaur on the ass gripped me so hard my feet started to move.

"Stop it!"

"Eris, whatever you're doing, stop," I heard Persephone's voice say, and mercifully my feet stilled. The grin on Eris' face vanished.

"Of course, oh Queen of dull," Eris said with an over the top bow. For a moment I thought her huge boobs would spill out of her top, but she straightened in time. "Good luck surviving my idiot brother, sweetie," she said to me, then turned and strode away.

"Thanks. You keep rescuing me," I said, turning gratefully to Persephone.

"Not for much longer. You're needed," she said.

She walked me the length of the room to stand in front of the dais with the thrones, Hades now occupying one. Ares glared at me as I approached, and as before, his anger seemed to steel me rather than intimidate me. I could take his bullshit. I gave him a potent 'fuck-off' look as I came to a stop beside him.

The other gods' eyes bore into me too, and I avoided looking at any of them directly. I wasn't one to shy away from threats, but damn - they were intimidating. Energy thrummed from them, swirling through the air like heat over tarmac. It was weird. And I didn't like it.

The smell of the ocean washed over me suddenly, so strong I froze, then a cool breeze seemed to cut through the uncomfortable power-heat. I felt myself relax instantly, and a man shimmered into being just in front of the dais.

He looked like a completely normal man in his sixties, with a weather-beaten face, fierce blue eyes, and a pale green toga. Persephone and Ares bowed on either side of me, so I did the same.

"Oceanus," ground out Ares as he straightened, and I felt my eyebrow quirk. This was the most powerful being in Olympus? But he didn't exude power like the gods behind him. All he exuded, in fact, was a cheerful calm.

"Ares," Oceanus said pleasantly. "I am pleased to hear that you may have an opportunity to prove yourself a true ruler." Every muscle in the God of War's body tensed, and I wished I could see under his helmet. I was pretty sure his face would be as red as a tomato. He clearly didn't like Oceanus much.

"I have agreed to help Hades with his escaped demon," he said eventually, voice hoarse.

"And in doing so, you will also be helping this young lady whose power you covet. How selfless." Oceanus' eyes twinkled as he looked at me, and I instantly trusted him. Which was very unlike me. I folded my arms, suspicious.

Oceanus smiled. "I have a desire to prove myself an ally to the Olympians," he said loudly, and turned in a full circle, looking at all the gods on their thrones in turn. "So I have a gift for you. It is in everyone's interest to get Ares back to ruling his... unique realm. But I am bound by my own rules, and those do not allow me to just hand out power of that magnitude. Power must be earned. It is the most dangerous thing in the world."

Silence met his words. Ares shifted, his armor clinking.

"If you return to Hades with both the escaped demon and the missing Guardians, then I will forge you a Trident of power."

No silence this time. Loud gasps rang through the room, and all of the gods behind him moved in their seats.

"I..." Ares began, then faltered. "A true Trident of power?"

"Yes. You will be restored to full strength."

"I accept," said Ares, bowing his head. I looked between the two men, blinking.

"Then you must be on your way."

Before I could think another thing, light flashed around me.

"Where the fuck are we now? And what is a Trident of power?" I said, anger getting the better of me as I blinked into bright sunlight and turned to Ares' hulking form. We were standing on sand, and all I could see behind him and around us was more sand. Piles of rocks and hardy plants that clearly refused to die in the desert heat dotted the landscape.

"We are in my realm. A Trident of power is extremely rare and grants its wielder power equal to that of an Olympian." Ares answered stiffly. The bright light was reflecting off his armor, making it hard to look at him, and for the first time I got an idea of what he might look like if he had his power and was truly godly. Except that he didn't have his power and he wasn't godly. He was an asshole.

"What do we do now?"

"We find the demon."

"Just like that? But we don't even have any supplies!"

"We don't need supplies, foolish mortal."

I scowled at him. "I don't give a flying fuck if you don't eat, but I sure do."

He let out a long, agitated breath. "Of course I eat. But I can use your power to flash us to food at any point," he growled. I paused, dropping my hands from my hips.

"Oh. Good. Because you don't want to see me hangry."

"What is hangry?"

I rolled my eyes. "Pray you don't find out," I muttered. He stared at me a moment through his stupid shiny helmet's eye slits.

"You are an idiot, and will likely get us killed," he said eventually.

"I'm not an idiot," I replied. Which was partially true. I couldn't argue the bit about getting us killed though. "And anyway, I thought you wanted me dead?"

"That depends," he said, turning and looking out over the nothingness.

"On what?"

"How irritating you are, and if you are at risk of killing me along with you."

Well, I was dead then. If I irritated him even half as much as he annoyed me, we were fucked.

There was a slightly pink shimmer in the air between us, and Ares froze, hand on his sword.

"I need to attend to some business before we embark upon this quest. I shall return shortly," he said, then vanished in a flash of pink.

5

ARES

"Who the hell does that washed up old has-been think he is!" I raged, stamping my foot against the marble of Aphrodite's throne room floor as I paced. The pink shimmer was her calling card, and I had been relieved to see it. I had expected her to want to see me before I left on my quest. I had *wanted* her to want to see me.

"Come now, Oceanus is hardly a has-been. And I think he's quite attractive," purred Aphrodite from her throne.

"Don't test me," I growled, turning to her. She gave me a sultry smile and all my damned resolve seeped from me as her beauty took over my senses. "Aphrodite, stop using your power on me," I demanded. "I can't withstand it with none of my own." Her smile vanished.

"I know, and I'm becoming bored. You're like a wolf with no fangs."

Anger, not with her but with myself, leaped

through me, but none of my godly power accompanied it. It was just plain, useless fury.

How could I have been so fucking careless? How had I let Zeus take my power?

"I have a way to get my strength back now," I told her, my voice harsh.

"Yes. A Trident of power. How exciting." She didn't sound excited. She sounded completely uninterested. "You know, you could just kill the girl."

"I would love to kill the girl. She is infuriating. But I would still have to carry out Hades' bidding and find this damned demon. Why anger the new Lord of the Gods if I would have to perform the same task regardless?"

Aphrodite sighed, and lifted a peach from the bowl of fruit that was always next to her throne.

"I suppose," she said. "But you never used to care about angering Lords. In fact, you quite enjoyed it."

"Petty little Lords in my own realm, yes. Not Hades."

Her smile slid back into place. It was breathtaking. *She* was breathtaking.

"Well, now those Lords will get a chance to get even with you," she said. Trepidation rippled through me, and I cursed my loss of power for the millionth time. Trepidation was not something I was familiar, or comfortable with.

But the Goddess of Love was right. When the Lords of War caught up with me, they would likely be stronger than I was. Unless the girl came into her power fast and I could use it all, as I hoped.

My eyes raked over my lover's smile.

"You take pleasure in my plight?" I snarled at her.

"Yes, Ares, I do. It's your own stupidity that got you here."

Her words struck me like a dagger. They were true. But to know she enjoyed my pain...

"Then I will leave you," I said stiffly.

"No. You will do as you came here to do. You will take pleasure in my body, and I yours, before you set off on this boring quest."

She still wanted me. The knowledge buoyed me, and I slowly pulled my helmet off. I saw the gleam in her eyes, before she flicked her hand.

"On second thoughts, I'm tired. I'll see you when you return from Aries. If you return."

I felt my face burn, and rammed my helmet back onto my head. I could not even flash myself out of her blasted fucking throne room. I had no power.

With another flick of her hand I was back in my desert, dismissed.

6

BELLA

"You left me alone in a fucking desert less than five minutes into this damned quest!" I yelled, when Ares appeared out of nowhere on the sand beside me just ten minutes after he had left.

The giant god looked at me long enough for me to register the fury in his dark eyes, then roared, drawing his sword from its sheath.

I ducked into a low crouch, balling my fists, the red mist descending fast.

But Ares turned, and I rose slowly as he started smashing his sword into a large cluster of boulders as though they had just announced themselves his mortal enemy. He bellowed with rage as he landed his weapon again and again on the rocks, and they cracked and crumbled under his wrath.

"Your business went well then?" I muttered, the red mist leaking away. I cocked my head as I watched him hacking the shit out of the rocks, his sound of his armor moving and the steel clash of his sword ringing though the air.

Whilst it was quite amusing to see his fury with the inanimate objects, I was also reluctantly impressed. Power or no power, the man could wield a sword. I mean, a pile of rocks wasn't the ideal target but... I'd destroyed enough plasterboard walls that didn't really deserve it in my time to withhold judgment.

I wondered absently what had made him so mad as I flopped back down on my ass with a sigh. If we really did share the same temper, then it didn't matter what had set him off, as long as I let him take it all out on the rocks. Especially since I was unarmed. Which was the first of a number of things I had decided needed resolving fast.

He'd only been gone for ten minutes, but that was long enough to be completely alone in a strange place, and for the panic I'd so far kept subdued to make some headway.

I had been abducted by the God of War and taken to a world that by all rights shouldn't exist. It probably said a lot about me that until I was alone and unarmed, a secret little part of me had actually been excited by that. Something in my life finally felt right, even if it was kind of impossible, and my friend's life was in danger.

As long as the adrenaline was burning through me I could eliminate anything that made me weak, any self-doubt or emotion that wasn't helpful. But standing in a damned desert with nothing at all did the opposite of that. Worry had begun crashing through me unchecked, a whirlwind of doubt and the undeniable truth that I was in way, way over my head smashing into me like a wrecking ball. The reality of my whole life changing in one day, being wanted dead by a violent god and now being expected to chase down a demon escaped from the Underworld finally hit me. And in a world where everyone was armed with dirty great swords or freaking magic, I was woefully under-equipped.

At that point in my runaway-train of panicked thoughts I had managed to latch onto something and steady myself. Weapons. I needed a weapon. With something nice and violent to focus on, I'd sat down on the hot sand, taken a deep breath, and forced myself to concentrate.

Joshua had once told me that list-making was a good way to feel in charge of a situation that otherwise felt out of my control. At the time this had seemed like good advice for when I lost yet another job, or my fuckwit landlord put my rent up for no good reason. But now that I knew Joshua was some sort of magic person from another damned world, I had to wonder under what circumstances he had really intended his advice to be used. It probably wasn't sat in a desert somewhere in Olympus trying to keep a panic attack at bay. None-the-less, I had made myself a list entitled 'things I need to survive in the realm of war'.

As Ares yelled again, his huge sword running out of rocks to smash, another stab of betrayal bit at me.

Joshua had known I was different the whole time. He had known I really didn't belong, and that it wasn't a damned chemical imbalance. He had tried to help me believe that I was normal, instead of just telling me why I'd always felt so out of place, so trapped. So wrong for the world I was in.

I squashed the feeling with a snort, and went through my list again in my head. There was no point getting myself worked up about Joshua until I had at least saved his life. I could yell at him for lying to me after that.

When Ares finally stomped back to me, his shoulders were heaving and his sword hung limply from his right arm.

"Better?" I asked him.

"No. Let's go."

"Woahhhh there," I said, springing to my feet. "You got to take care of some business, so I think it's only fair that I do too."

"Your business is inconsequential," he said. I bit down on my tongue, hard. I would not swear at him. I needed his co-operation.

"It would make life a lot easier for both of us if I had a change of clothes and some of my stuff," I said calmly.

"Why do you need more clothes?" he scowled.

"Because I like to change my fucking underwear every now and then!" So much for not swearing.

"Use magic," he shrugged.

"I don't know how to."

"Then I shall do it."

"Not a chance in sweet freaking hell are you going anywhere near my underwear!"

"As if I-" he started angrily, but I held up my hands and spoke over him as loudly as I could.

"Just take me to my apartment so I can throw some stuff in a backpack, or I'll give you endless shit until you do. It's that simple, armor-boy."

I knew I would win eventually, and I was right. But I wasn't prepared for the feeling I got when Ares finally flashed us back to my apartment and I stared around at the dimly-lit space. A pang of something strong gripped me, and it wasn't sadness or fondness for my home. It was a gut-wrenching delight at the thought that I might never have to see the place again.

It may have been a little premature, but I was quite sure that whatever the hell was happening to me was the start of something that did *not* end with me returning to this dump.

"You live here?" Ares' tone held a note of disbelief, and something else I couldn't identify. Probably general assholery, I decided as I made my way quickly through my tiny kitchen, into my tinier bedroom. I was lucky to have a separate bedroom at all, living this close to the city center, but that didn't mean I liked the place. The neighbors were awful, always yelling at each other, fighting and throwing stuff that banged off the walls and set my temper humming. And everything was damp. The shitty landlord never fixed anything he was asked to, and no matter how much mold-removing product I covered the minuscule shower-room in, dark slimy mildew always crept back over the walls and ceiling in a matter of hours.

"Where do you sit, or eat?" Ares called as I pulled up the thin single mattress on my bed to get to the storage space beneath it.

I ignored him, finding an old khaki-colored back-pack and yanking it out. The answer was that I ate sitting on the bed, the bare walls closing in around me as I tried to watch Netflix or read on my phone. I was an outdoors kind of girl, and ADHD levels of hyperactivity meant I was ill-suited to a space this cramped. But I couldn't afford more. Hell, right now I couldn't even afford this. The only saving grace of the entire building was the basement. It had been slowly filled over the years with tired but functional second-hand gym gear, including a punch-bag. I couldn't pay for real gym membership, so even though it had no ventilation and got hotter than the freaking sun down there under the four-story concrete building, I never uttered a bad word about it. I *needed* it.

I started to throw t-shirts, two pairs of jeans, and a whole pile of socks and underwear into the bag, barely paying attention to what I was selecting. Other than my Guns N' Roses t-shirt. I made sure I had that. I slipped off my sneakers and shoved them into the bag, pulling my only decent-quality shoes on in their place. They were whacking great big walking boots, with hidden steel-caps, that did some serious damage to whatever they connected with.

Then I pulled open the drawer in the little unit by my bed and wrapped my hand around the thing I had really come for. My flick-blade. It may not be as big as Ares' sword, but the little knife and I had history, and it had never let me down. No way was I facing Underworld demons without it. Or hulking armored giants with no sense of humor.

"I am glad you came back here."

I jumped so hard in surprise that the blade slipped from my fingers and landed on the threadbare carpet.

"Zeeva!" The bastard cat appeared on my bed, her tail swishing.

"You are aware you are unlikely to see this place again?"

"Yes, and good riddance," I said, picking up my knife, pulse slowing.

"I mean London, not this awful apartment," she said, her mental voice laden with distaste.

I faltered. I wouldn't miss this shithole, but London? The city was special.

"Does Olympus have musicals?" I asked hopefully.

"Olympus has plays beyond your wildest dreams, but I doubt you shall ever see them," she answered.

"Why not?"

"Primarily because I would be surprised if you survive Ares and his realm," she said bluntly. I scowled at her. *"But even if you do, you can't stay in Olympus."*

A sick feeling churned through my stomach. The only reason I wasn't completely freaking out was that

Olympus felt so right, even though I'd barely spent an hour there.

"Why can't I stay?"

"You are of the mortal world now. You need power to live in Olympus if you are not raised there."

"I have power! That's why Ares wants me!"

"But you can't use it yourself." Her tone was that of every teacher I had ever known when I failed to do what I had been asked, and at that moment I realized what she was doing. She was goading me.

"You want me to learn to use my power?" I asked. Her amber eyes flicked to the door, where Ares stood beyond.

"He will not teach you. You may only rely on yourself."

"Can you teach me?" She bared her needle-like teeth.

"Your power could not be more different than mine. I can teach you nothing."

I didn't think that was true, given that I knew fuck all. When you were starting from zero, anything at all was more than nothing.

"Well, as it happens, 'learn magic war power' was next on my list, right after 'arm myself'," I said haughtily. Her eyes moved to my knife, safely folded shut as I pushed it into my jeans pocket.

When she said nothing else, I grabbed my deodorant and a few other bits from the hanging shelves in my washroom, then zipped up my bag, mentally crossing the items off the packing list I'd made in the desert.

"You know, I might not *want* to stay in Olympus," I

lied, as I slung one strap of the backpack over my shoulder and looked at the cat. She blinked slowly.

"You want to stay," she said. *"As a true goddess, you could explore a world that is truly limitless. Realms that float in the sky, reside in volcanoes, are submerged in golden domes in the ocean. Ships that soar through the sky. Magic that can provide endless experiences, tastes, feelings, desires. People, gods and creatures that will obliterate the boundaries of your imagination. Stories that will leave you desperate for more. And adventures that will never end if you do not want them to."*

The bag slipped off my shoulder as my muscles went slack. Zeeva was describing my greatest dream. A world where I could not get bored. Where my boundless energy and vivid imagination could be constantly absorbed. My eyes were glazing over as I imagined it, my drab, moldy, tiny apartment vanishing behind a vision of freedom and life.

"And I can only stay if I have magic?" I breathed.

"Yes." The vision cleared abruptly, my mushroom-colored walls slamming back down around me.

The idea of actually having or using magic was something my brain had so far refused to dwell on. The fact that I had heard my own apparent War power referenced countless times in the last crazy few hours didn't make it feel any more real or true.

I mean, it wasn't like I didn't believe it. Why the hell would Ares have shown up in my life otherwise?

But I didn't feel like I had any magic power. And as arrogant as it might have been, I had enough confidence in my ability as a scrappy but pretty accomplished fighter to not *have* to process the idea. I could survive without magic, I was sure, so I was focusing on Joshua, and arming myself. Things I knew about, could work with and control.

But if I ultimately needed the magic to stay in Olympus... That changed things. That was a motivation I could use, that I could force my brain to accept. I'd show that stuck-up cat I could learn magic.

If Ares could use it, then so could I.

I just had to find a way of getting him to tell me where to start.

7

BELLA

When I stepped back into my kitchen, which somewhat impossibly looked even smaller with the enormous god squished into it, Ares grunted and locked his eyes on mine. The red plume of his helmet was flattened against the grubby ceiling, and I failed to suppress a smirk. He looked ridiculous.

"Why do you live here?"

"It's all I could afford that came with a free punch-bag."

"Afford? You pay money to reside in this... box?"

"Jeez, you're clueless. Yes, armor-boy, I pay money to live here. Is Olympus rent-free?" The last question came out more hopefully than sarcastic.

Ares shifted his weight, looking disdainfully at my splintered gray cupboards. "In my realm you live under the rules of your Lord or King."

"And how do your Lords and Kings become Lords and Kings?"

Ares shrugged and the metal of his helmet scraped the ceiling at the same time his shoulder plates clanged against the kitchen unit. "The Lords are deities; they are born that way. They delegate power to the Kings."

"You got any Queens?" I asked. He nodded.

"Many. Hippolyta of the Amazons is my favorite." His eyes lit up as he spoke her name, and I remembered Persephone saying that that she was his daughter. The thought made me uncomfortable, so although this was the most amicable and useful conversation we'd had so far, I changed the subject.

"You ready to go? I need to find my friend." Ares' eyes darkened.

"Always you talk about your friend," he grumbled.

"Yes. That's generally what friends do. They give a shit. Do you have tequila in Olympus?" I asked, spying the bottle of booze on the counter behind him, next to the broken kettle.

"What is tequila?"

"My version of nectar of the gods," I muttered, swiping the bottle and tipping my bag forward to open it. When the tequila was safely stowed inside, I put my hands on my hips, and cast my eyes around the little apartment one last time. There was nothing at all that I would miss here. Which in itself was sad. But it only served to strengthen my resolve. I couldn't be more ready to move on, even if it was to something mostly unbelievable and very likely lethal. "Let's go."

∼

"So... Why are we starting here, in the empty desert?" I asked when the light from the flash cleared from my eyes and I clocked my sandy surroundings again.

"Stop talking," Ares grunted.

"Hey, if I'm going to do this with you then you have to tell me what's going on," I said, as he began to stomp through the sand. "I'm not going to just follow you about like a damned puppy."

"If you want to survive, and find your godsforsaken friend, then you will do exactly that." He paused and turned to look at me, something malicious gleaming in his eyes. "You will behave like my pet."

Anger, hot and real, flushed through me. "Your pet?" I echoed, my voice low.

"Correct." He nodded, his stupid helmet plume bouncing.

"I am nobody's fucking pet," I growled. The red mist slammed down, energy soaring through my veins, filling my muscles.

"You will start by swearing less," he said.

"I will start by ripping your freaking head off, you overgrown jerk!"

I leaped at him before I could stop myself, and cried out as I hit an invisible wall, bouncing back and landing hard on my ass. Dusty sand flew up around me as I scrabbled to my feet. *Never stay down longer than you need to.* Ares folded his arms, self-satisfied.

But before I could try flinging myself at him again, I realized something. It wasn't just my shoulder and hip that had physically felt that wall of power. Something in my gut had too.

With a roar, I launched myself at him again, but dropped low at the last minute, aiming to swipe out his legs. I hit the invisible barrier again, as I expected, but this time I was concentrating. There it was! A flare of something, like a sharp yank on a cord deep in my belly. Was that him accessing my power?

I yelped as I was suddenly lifted off my ass, my distraction by the alien feeling giving Ares the upper-hand. Literally. He had my shirt in his fist like he'd scruffed a dog, and was picking me up off the ground. I struggled and thrashed, half-expecting my shirt to tear, but he set me back down surprisingly gently. I turned to glare up at him, and he glared back. He was at least two feet taller than me.

"Stop wasting time," he said.

"Stop being a prick," I replied. Sparks flew in his dark eyes, and I was close enough to see that they looked like burning embers. They were... much more interesting to look at than they should be. I snapped my eyes away.

"Why are you making this so difficult?"

"Oh, I don't know, probably because you introduced yourself with your intention to kill me? Or maybe because you don't give a flying fuck about saving Joshua and are only doing this to save your own ass? Or perhaps it's just because you're a humorless oaf."

"The fastest way to save your friend is to stop angering me," he said, and there was a new, very real strain in his voice.

"Tell me how to use my power," I said, finding his eyes again.

"No," he answered flatly, and turned around, resuming his stride.

"Then I'll keep being a pain in the ass," I said, almost jogging to catch up with him.

"You will do that regardless," he spat. I couldn't really argue with that, so I reluctantly fell in beside him. The adrenaline from my brief and unsuccessful bout with him was still churning through me, firing me up, but the red mist had melted away. The fastest way to help Joshua was to keep moving, not uselessly attack Ares.

"At least tell me where we're going," I said.

"We are going to one of Aries' busiest cities, to find out who knows anything of this accursed demon," he sighed, after a long pause.

"Oh." I said. That seemed like a good idea, but I wasn't going to tell him that. "Why aren't we flashing there?"

"Because the King of Erimos does not allow flashing into his city. Only out."

I moved my curiosity about Erimos and its king to a new list called 'things to ask about later'. "But if you're the god of this realm, can't you just break the rules?"

Ares took a long breath, then let it out slowly. I got the distinct impression he felt like he was talking to a child.

"Your power is a shadow of what mine was. It will strengthen the longer you are here, but right now, the most impressive thing that you can do is flash." I opened my mouth indignantly to defend my newly discovered magic, but Ares continued before I could speak. "Many in the cities of my realm would choose to take advantage of me, should they discover my lack of strength. To topple the God of War would be a legendary feat. So we shall not be revealing my identity to anyone."

A little ripple of excitement took me, and I really wasn't sure why. "You're going to move through your own realm in disguise?"

"I can see no other way." He did not sound happy about it at all, but for some reason, I was thrilled with the idea. It was like being in a spy movie or something. Maybe it was my love of theater, and the opportunity I was about to be given to be a real actress that was so exciting. Or maybe I was just more messed up than I realized I was.

"Won't they recognize you? You're pretty, erm... distinctive." I eyed his hulking frame as I asked the question. Ares said nothing, just stamped across the barren desert, his armor clinking. "Are you going to use magic to change what you look like?" I tried again.

"Your power is not strong enough for me to use it for a prolonged period like that. It would drain you and render you unconscious." I didn't like the lilt of happiness in his voice at the mention of me being unconscious.

"Then how are you going to disguise yourself? Surely everyone knows what you look like?"

Ares slowed to a stop, putting his huge fists on his hips.

"You have no idea how little I want to do this," he said quietly. "With you of all people."

"Do what?" A combination of apprehension and excitement skittered over my skin in the warm desert heat. What was he about to do?

"There are only three beings who have ever seen my face." I barely heard the words from behind his helmet, he spoke so low.

"Why?"

"The helmet of war is part of me. You would not understand." My mind jumped to my knife, and how wrong I felt when I didn't have it, but I dismissed the thought, concentrating on Ares.

"So, you never take it off?"

"Not in front of people, no."

"Are you really ugly?" I couldn't help the question, and his head snapped to me, embers in his furious eyes again.

"You mock me?" I swore I could hear the actual ring of steel in his words, and there was a tiny tug in my tummy. *I was making him mad enough to use my magic again.*

"It's just a helmet," I shrugged.

"You are an ignorant, selfish, weak child," he growled, the embers growing and coloring his eyes a dancing amber. I took a breath, the sight utterly mesmerizing. The longer I looked at the fire burning in his eyes, the more I was sure I could hear the ringing of swords and distant drums, the more the sensation of being flooded with adrenaline and the unbeatable feeling of victory tingled through me. He must have mistaken my awe for fear though, because his shoulders squared and he took a step back, giving a small, satisfied nod and breaking the spell.

Deciding that it was probably safer to let him think that I was scared of him than let him know he had the most beautiful eyes I'd ever seen, I kept my mouth shut, but residual tingling still pulsed across my skin. This was not what I needed. At all. But already I wanted to see the fire in his eyes again.

He just called you a weak child! Not cool! Get it together, Bella, I chided myself mentally.

"If I'm ignorant, then that's your fault. You won't tell me anything." I folded my arms across my chest, the tingling finally ebbing away.

Ares shifted his weight from one foot to the other, armor jangling. "I will tell you what you need to know about Erimos on the way," he offered eventually.

"I'm not interested in Erimos," I said, although I totally was. "I want to know why you're so attached to this helmet. Do you sleep with it?"

Ares gave a bark of annoyance, this time stamping his foot on the ground. "You are everything I hate about humans!"

"I'm going to take that as a compliment, on behalf of all humans," I said. Truth was, I didn't think I represented humans well at all, they mostly seemed to hate me. But he didn't need to know that.

"The helmet was a gift from my father," he snapped.

"Zeus? The same Zeus who stole your power?"

"Yes."

"Don't you hate him now?"

"No. He is mighty and strong and our true leader."

"Then... Why'd he take your power?" I felt the tug in my tummy before I saw Ares begin to grow, his armor shining and growing with him. My eyes went straight to his, with a spark of hope. *I wanted to see the fire.*

"My father will have had his reasons. And I will have an eternity to work them out. In the meantime, we will find this blasted demon, get your accursed friend, and deliver them to Hades!"

"And show the whole of your realm your real face," I added, with a small shrug.

A blast of power erupted from the god, and before I could blink, I was tumbling backwards. Heat and the sound of drums engulfed me as I lost my footing, but then my butt bounced off something soft, righting me on my feet again. I had my arms flung out, trying to regain sturdy footing as I looked up at Ares. Embers burned in his chocolate eyes and the stupid tingles started up again instantly. I could still hear the drums.

"You are impossible," he snarled. "Are you trying to force me to lose my temper?"

"No," I lied. *A little.* Though I knew how stupid that was. He probably would kill me.

I turned my head to see what had broken my fall, but there was nothing there. Had I somehow used my magic? Or had Ares stopped me falling on my ass again? I couldn't imagine he cared much about my ass though.

"Removing my helmet will be the hardest thing I have done in centuries. If you can't respect that, keep your mouth closed," he said quietly.

To my utter astonishment, his words actually made me feel guilty. If this really was such a big deal for him, maybe I should back off a little. *But he was going to kill you!* My indignant inner voice was right, but I couldn't bring myself to goad him again. Centuries was a long time. Plus, there was a curious part of me that wanted to see what he looked like under the armor.

In a flash, my sex-starved brain served me an image of him, under the metal. And I mean under *all* of the metal. Huge, hulking, and *naked*. I couldn't stop the heat spreading across my cheeks and blinked the image away quickly. Weirdly, naked Ares in my head still had the helmet on. It seemed it was easier for my imagination to conjure up a naked body than to invent the god's face. Bet a shrink would have fun with that one.

When I did indeed keep my mouth shut, Ares huffed an angry breath, and turned his back to me, taking a few long strides and putting a decent distance between us. I almost made a quip about him being a drama queen and clamped my jaw shut tightly to stop the words escaping.

But geez, the man was over-dramatic. What was he hiding under there? An image of Shrek popped into my head and I bit back a snort of laughter slightly too late. Ares tossed me an angry glare over his shoulder, then gripped the bottom of his helmet.

Anticipation skittered through me, unbidden. Why did I care what he looked like? He lifted his hands, pulling the helmet clear from his head. A mass of warm brown, slightly wavy hair fell down his back, and my eyebrows shot up in surprise. It was streaked through with white and reached well past his massive shoulders. I watched wide-eyed as he dropped the helmet onto the sand and began to tie it back into a tail with a leather strap. I really would not have guessed him as a long-hair-kinda-guy. In fact, I would have staked money on him being an angry-buzz-cut-kinda-guy.

When he finally turned to me, it took every ounce of willpower I possessed to keep my jaw from dropping.

Fuck me sideways, Ares was hot. Hot enough that this was the most evidence I had had so far that he wasn't actually human. No human looked like that.

Those chocolate brown eyes that stormed with fire were set in a face that could not have blended stern and sexy any better. His hard, angular cheekbones and jawline were offset by full soft lips, and his short, dark beard somehow made his wavy hair look intensely more masculine. He was perfect. Simply perfect.

"Well, I guess you won't need a paper bag," I breathed.

He frowned, dark eyebrows drawing together. "Why would anyone need a bag made of paper?"

Seeing his mouth move as he spoke for the first time gave me an inexorable desire to feel his soft lips, and I screwed my face up. *He was a god. Of course he would be hot. That didn't mean he wasn't still an asshole! Focus!*

"It's just an expression from my world," I said, shaking my head. "What are you going to do with that?" I asked, pointing to his helmet in the sand.

"I will hide it, along with this." He banged a fist on his massive chest-plate, and my cheeks burned as though someone was holding a flame to them. Great. The hottest asshole I'd ever met was about to undress.

I tried to distract myself by sitting and doodling in the sand, whilst Ares clanged about, removing his armor. *Joshua*. This was about saving Joshua, I told myself repeatedly, drawing a large spiral with my finger. I needed to stop delaying Ares and get a move on. As soon as he was ready to go, I'd start behaving myself; rein in the attitude, and focus.

"Let's go," Ares grunted, snapping me out of my self-scolding. I leaped to my feet, pulling my bag with me, then stumbled as I turned to the god. He was wearing simple black linen pants, and no freaking shirt.

"Why aren't you wearing a shirt?" I fixed my gaze on his face, his outrageously sculpted pecs burning into my lower peripheral vision.

"People in Erimos do not wear shirts," he answered simply.

"The women better wear damned shirts," I said, alarmed. I wasn't walking into an alien city with my boobs out. Not a chance.

Ares gave me a look as though I was ten years old. "It is clear you are a tourist. You may stay dressed as you are." Across his forehead was a gold band, the same material as his shining helmet. I pointed to it.

"Is that your armor? In disguise?" He nodded. "Neat trick," I said, impressed. "But you do look a little... regal."

He rolled his eyes and turned his back to me,

striding through the sand. It was entirely impossible not to look at his massive shoulders, the way his toned muscles moved as he walked, the dimples in the small of his back. The low waistline of his pants... I gave myself a hard mental slap. *No more ogling, Bella. It's time to find Joshua.*

8

BELLA

We'd only spent about a minute walking, in complete and awkward silence, when a teal shimmer caught my attention, and I slowed to a stop. Zeeva appeared on the sand before me, gave a languid cat stretch, then sat neatly, tail wrapped around herself.

"Why is your cat here?" growled Ares, stopping and turning to glare at us both.

"Beats me," I shrugged, refusing to look at his bare chest. His muscular, tanned, hulking bare chest. "What's up, Zeeva?"

"I assume you are headed for Erimos?" she asked in my head. I nodded. She yawned.

"Unfortunately, my tether to you will not work once you are in the city. I must stay with you now."

"Oh." I didn't really know if I wanted her with me or not. She hadn't exactly been friendly or helpful so far. But she did know more than me, and I supposed her presence couldn't hurt. I looked up at Ares. "She's coming with us to Erimos," I told him.

Ares snarled. "You are not welcome, spy," he hissed at Zeeva. I didn't hear her reply to him, but he looked pissed as he stamped a leather boot, then turned and resumed his march, his delicious back somehow radiating anger.

"Well, you managed to piss him off again," I said to the cat. She didn't bother to answer me, just sauntered after him.

"So, you were going to tell me about Erimos," I prompted when I caught up with them. I was getting hot, but I hadn't brought any water, only tequila, which on reflection wasn't very helpful in a desert.

"It is run by a particularly brutal king. There are fighting pits all over my realm, and he has the largest, and the most, gambling establishments. Erimos has money. Many come here to enjoy drink and women." Ares barked the words, a hum of anger still rolling from him.

"Lovely," I said. "What's a fighting pit?"

"*A gladiator ring, in your world,*" Zeeva's voice sounded in my head, at the same time Ares shook his head.

"You are clueless," he muttered.

"You don't think that's where Joshua has been taken, do you?" All misplaced sexual thoughts about

Ares vanished as images of Joshua chained up and forced to fight gladiators filled my mind.

Ares just shrugged. "If a demon has been spotted in my realm, someone in Erimos will know about it," he said. "That is why we are going there."

Anxiety pulsed through me, the reality check sharpening my focus.

"Your friend is a Guardian, not a fighter. It is unlikely he would have been taken to the pits," Zeeva said a long few moments later. I looked at her gratefully, but she didn't turn to me.

"How do I talk back to you in my head?" I asked her.

"Just concentrate on projecting the words to me alone. But I'd really rather you didn't. You're annoying enough already."

"Charming," I muttered. Even in Olympus, nobody fucking liked me, not even my own damned cat.

I could kind of see their point though, I thought glumly as we walked across the sand, the vista around us still void of anything except the odd scrubby bush or pile of rocks. I just wasn't good at staying still, or relaxing. I put people on edge, irritated them. And that was the best-case scenario. I'd lost many friends just through the kind of trouble I seemed to attract. Or more honestly, I lost them when they saw my *reaction* to the kind of trouble I attracted. I couldn't walk away from a fight. I couldn't back down when challenged. I couldn't just work out what was best for me and make a smart decision. I ran on pure impulse and energy. And it scared people. Hell, sometimes it scared me.

"We are here. I know it will be hard but try to keep

your mouth closed and let me speak," Ares said abruptly, turning away.

I frowned around us at the endless sand. "Erm, is the city invisible?"

Ares looked at me like I was mental. "Invisible? And you have the nerve to call me an oaf." He shook his head yet again, then frightened the living shit out of me by bellowing so loudly I thought he'd been stabbed or something.

"What in the name of-" I started, but my shout was drowned out instantly by the sound of roaring wind, and my hair whipped up into my face as the sand around us began to spin into peaked tornadoes. Within seconds I could see nothing but the beige of the sand whirling around us, and even though there seemed to be a pocket of clear air surrounding the three of us, panic surged through me, instinct taking over. But as fast as the sandstorm had started, it stopped. The sand didn't fall back to earth like it should though, spinning off into the sky and disappearing into clouds instead. I looked back down to see that the sand had left a massive sunken clearing in its place, filled with the most magnificent walled city I could have possibly imagined.

My immediate impression was that it looked like Agrabah from the Disney movie Aladdin. But as I looked closer at the jewel encrusted walls that surrounded the shining metropolis before us, I began to notice the darker details. Skulls were set between the pale stone and the jewels, and the bulbous spires on the buildings that peaked high above the walls were

decorated with swirling carvings of weapons. Swords
and flails and axes and hammers were all intricately
entwined in huge patterns across the impressive archi-
tecture.

From our elevated position I could see that the
grand spired towers were mostly in the middle of the
square city, and the further toward the walls I looked,
the smaller the buildings became. But they were all
made of the same stone, and they all glittered in the
sun, as though wealth was built into the structures
themselves. Broad courtyards filled with fabric
marquees occupied the spaces between the buildings,
and I could just make out figures bustling around.
Surrounding the city, beyond the walls, were six or
seven sunken pits lined with rows of stepped benches,
with circular stages in the center. *The fighting pits,* I realized with a pang of morbid curiosity. Between the pits
were hundreds of brightly colored tents in clusters and
I frowned at them.

"Why are they outside the city?" I asked, pointing at
the tents.

"You must pay to enter Erimos. The people who live
in those tents can't afford to go inside the walls." Ares
stamped down the sandy dune, and I followed him.

"I'm guessing you have money?" I asked, suddenly
aware of how penniless I was. Ares just grunted.

"They use drachma here." I looked down at Zeeva, the
cat seeming to almost float across the sand, effortlessly
graceful.

"Right. Good to know," I said, even though it meant
nothing to me at all. But I would take any and all of the

information offered to me. Eventually some of it would surely be useful.

When we got to the bottom of the dune, the gates of Erimos loomed large and imposing in front of us. Up close I could make out lots of bones embedded in the stone walls, not just the skulls visible from further away. Diamonds glittered amongst femurs, sapphires glinted against ribs, and amethysts shone around collarbones. It was creepy as hell, but I burned to explore a city such as this. It called to me.

But when he reached the intricate iron gates and the two armor-clad guards collecting coins from the trickle of folk moving through them, Ares turned left sharply, walking instead along the outside of the wall.

"Why aren't we going in?" I asked, walking fast to keep pace with him. The sounds of people calling out, selling wares and greeting each other died out as we moved further along the wall.

"We may be able to get the information we need without entering the city."

"But I want to enter the city!"

"I don't care what you want."

"Clearly," I snapped.

"He is avoiding the King of Erimos," offered Zeeva.

"Why?"

"Ask him."

"Why are you avoiding the King?" I asked Ares, and he turned sharply, snarling at the cat.

"Meddling beast," he hissed at her. She flicked her

tail. "He is not just a King. And it will be best if he does not know I am here."

"But you're in disguise."

"I will not take unnecessary risks!" he shouted, drawing to a stop and rounding on me. "This is my realm, my world, my rules, and you will stop challenging me!"

I glowered back at him, but stayed silent, remembering my resolve to behave. To an extent, he was right. At least about it being his world. He definitely knew best here, and the fastest way to get to Joshua was to let Ares do what he needed to do.

But there was no way I was playing by his rules.

It took another five minutes to reach one of the clusters of tents. I couldn't see the sunken fighting pit that I knew was just beyond the campsite because we were on level ground now, but my body hummed with curiosity.

"The people who live here are pit fighters. Many are owned by slavers who stay in the city," said Ares quietly as we got close.

"Why don't they run away?"

"Most are bound and cannot. But not all of them. Some fight for glory," he answered. "They are a hard people. Keep your mouth closed and let me talk."

The tents were all of the colors of a circus, bright reds, blues, purples and yellows, and their inhabitants looked just as colorful. I made a sincere effort to keep my interest from showing on my face as Ares slowed down and we walked casually into the camp. Directly ahead of us was a large fire, an iron pot swinging over it, and about six people were seated around it on wooden stools. As far as I could tell, they were all dressed similarly, shirtless with baggy hareem pants in purple or red. But that was where the similarities ended.

Two of them, I was pretty sure, were minotaurs. They were as tall as Ares, covered in dark fur, had hoofed feet and snouted faces, and most impressive of all had giant horns curling up out of their foreheads. They were freaking awesome. As the group began to notice our approach, a creature with loads of spikes sticking out of his bald head turned to us, and I saw that he only had one amber eye in the middle of his deformed face. He stood up, and I realized with a jolt that *he* was a *she*. A badly torn rag was tied around her chest, and she fixed her single eye on Ares.

"State your business," she said as the whole group stared at us. The other three men looked human. I plastered a friendly smile on my face, whilst adrenaline streamed through my system.

"My... friend is missing. I am seeking information," said Ares. The cyclops nodded, and he continued. "Have you heard anything about an Underworld demon moving through Erimos?"

The cyclops' face was an unmoving mask, and one of the minotaurs kicked at the iron pot, making it swing. A waft of something meaty-smelling washed over us.

"We have heard nothing of the sort."

"No new demons on the fighting circuit?"

"We can't help you." Her voice was hard, and Ares tensed. I felt a pull in my gut as anger rolled from him.

He was a god. He couldn't be used to people refusing him. I couldn't help wondering if anyone less powerful than him had ever refused him before.

"That smells good," I said, before he could lose his shit and give us away. "What is it?"

One of the human men gave me a pointed look up and down, then answered.

"Alexsis lost her leg in the pits last week. She died this morning."

"Oh. Sorry to hear that," I said, confused. Why was he telling me about his friend dying? The man shrugged.

"She was our cook. This is all we have left now that she's gone."

"Shit," I said sympathetically.

"Can you cook?" asked the minotaur closest to me. His voice was like a rake on gravel.

I barked out a laugh. "No. Unless you count grilled cheese." I felt another wave of power roll off Ares, and guessed it was now aimed at me. Time to shut my mouth. "Well, thanks for your help and good luck learning to cook," I said cheerily, starting to turn around.

All of five of them stood up in unison. I paused in my turn, and my muscles clenched as my instincts kicked in, strength surging through my body.

"We need a cook," growled the minotaur. "And that will feed us for a week." He pointed at Ares' headband.

"I told you that you looked too regal!" I hissed at

him. He looked at me, furious, and my words died on my lips. Embers burned across his irises. As if in direct response, the mist dropped over my own eyes. My vision sharpened even as it turned red, and the familiar feeling of being too large for my own body swamped me. My skin hummed with barely contained energy as I tore my eyes from Ares and turned back to the group.

"I'm not your fucking cook."

"We'll see about that, little lady," said one of the humans, then shimmered and morphed before my eyes into something... insane. It had the body of a panther, dark and sleek and powerful looking, and the glowing red tail of a scorpion was raised high over its back. Before my brain even had time to process that curveball, the thing snarled and launched itself at us.

As fast as lightning, Ares was between me and the thing, swinging his massive arm out as he side-stepped and dropped to his knees. His forearm slammed into the creature as it charged past him to get to me, and I felt a wrenching in my gut. The creature flew through the air like a freaking Frisbee. I watched open-mouthed as it crashed down into a tent thirty feet away, and shouts went up from inside.

"What the-" started the cyclops woman, but Ares cut her off with a roar as he charged towards the campfire. All sensible thought about escaping or not causing a scene abandoned me, and with a battle cry to match his, I threw myself in after him.

9

BELLA

I'd be lying if I said a part of me didn't enjoy the red mist. The thing about being a five-foot-two blonde with a big mouth is that people constantly underestimate you. And there are few things as satisfying as seeing their faces when they realize their mistake.

I went for the closest target to me, the minotaur who had suggested I'd be his cook. I slid my flick-knife from my pocket as I charged, my narrowing focus taking in his broadening stance and his snarling snout as I approached. I registered his shoulder moving as he drew back his arm and I turned up my speed, strength flooding my legs as I powered toward him. I managed to get under his elbow before he even realized how close I was, whipping out my hand and slashing at his rib cage. He let out a snorting bellow as my knife made contact and I pivoted on the balls of my feet, jabbing the blade back into anything I could reach. I got him square in the small of his back, and I forced as much of my anger-fueled strength into the jab as I could. It was enough to topple him, a cry of pain escaping his snout. But my elation was short lived. A wrenching in my stomach cut through my concentration completely, and I whirled to see the God of War picking up the cyclops by the neck, practically glowing with power. My peripheral vision clouded on one side and it was enough of a warning for me to just avoid the punch thrown at me by the other minotaur.

"What the hell did you do to him?" it said in a vaguely female voice. Prickles of guilt edged my anger, trying to derail my focus, but they couldn't get through. The focus was too strong.

"The same as I'm about to do to you," I hissed, drawing my knife back. But I didn't get a chance to do another thing because the cyclops came hurtling through the air, then smashed into the minotaur, both of them yelling as they crumpled to the sand. Ares had thrown the creature clear across the campfire clearing, into *my* minotaur.

"If I were you, I would leave now, before Ares gives you both away," said Zeeva's calm voice in my head.

"No way! We're just getting started," I answered her, throwing a glare at Ares, then looking around for the other two human men. They were nowhere to be seen. But movement registered on my right, and I saw the panther with the scorpion tail stalking through the tents toward us. I heard Ares snarl, and felt another pull in my gut, and my focus slipped again with the alien feeling. "Stop doing that!" I shouted, turning to the god. His eyes were dancing with red, gleaming with power.

"I have missed this," he breathed. Was he getting high off my war power?

"Well, you're putting me off!"

"I do not need your help."

A surge of anger bolstered me, an idea striking.

"Yes, you do. You're weak without me."

Exactly as I'd expected, I felt the tug in my tummy that accompanied Ares' anger at my words, but this time I turned my focus inward, and I tugged back.

He let out a shocked breath, then I felt a burst of *something* shoot through my hands, into my flick-blade. The weapon seared hot under my fingers, and the sound of war drums banged loud in my ears. Everything slowed around me, and it was like my normal fighting focus had been multiplied by a million. I could see what was happening around me in slow-motion. It was incredible. *I was invincible.*

Or at least, I would have been if I had eyes in the back of my head.

Pain lanced through my left shoulder blade, and the magical moment severed abruptly. I couldn't help the scream that tore from my lips as white-hot agony burned all the way down my spine, and my legs buckled. Sand flew up around me as I crashed to the ground, and my vision swam like I was underwater as I struggled to hold onto what was happening. I heard the drums redouble, a roar from Ares, the snarl of a cat, then my head hit the sand.

10

ARES

"I told you she would get us killed!" The girl was a dead-weight over my shoulder as I stamped through the entrance gates to Erimos. Nobody cast us a second glance. As long as you'd paid entry to the city you could be carrying five dead bodies on your back and no-one would care.

"*If you hadn't accessed her power so much, she wouldn't have been tempted to try to use it herself,*" Hera's accursed cat answered me. "*You were foolish to fight those men. You should have walked away.*"

"The God of War does not walk away from a fight," I spat.

"*And now the God of War can't access any power because his only source has been poisoned by a manticore,*" she sang back at me. I screwed my face up, a sick feeling churning through my gut. Gods, I wished I had my helmet on. It felt so completely wrong to have my face exposed like this. But other than a few appreciative looks from the local whores, I was largely being ignored.

I knew where the sole apothecary was in Erimos and turned left into the busiest of the many bazaars in the city. Hawkers shouting and the smell of spices consumed me as I strode through the square, Bella's cheek bouncing softly against the skin of my back as I walked. Something uneasy flashed through me again as I recalled her face changing from awe to shocked pain as the manticore stinger had sunk into her back. I'd barely had enough time to access her power and deal with the vile thing before she'd fallen unconscious. And as such, cutting off my access to her power.

That was where the uneasy feeling was coming from, I was sure. I was utterly powerless whilst she was like this. It was nothing to do with the fact that actual flames had burned in her eyes when she had looked at me in the camp, her muscles tense, her weapon ready.

She was rude, impulsive, unladylike, and embodied everything I disliked in a woman. She was the opposite of Aphrodite. So it did not matter that I had heard the drums of war when I looked into her eyes. What mattered was keeping her alive long enough to use her power to hunt down the escaped demon and getting my *own* blessed power back.

"She's blue," said the owner of the apothecary, when I slid the girl from over my shoulder onto the stone table in front of him. His store was lined with bottles of hundreds of colors. Some were so bright they made my eyes squint. Bowls of powders and ooze were interspersed with the bottles, and the whole place smelled like iron.

"I'm sure you've seen worse," I said.

"Hmmm," he responded, dipping his head to look at her face. He was a small human man, with thinning hair and spectacles. "Manticore sting?" He asked, looking at the blackening wound in her back.

"Yes."

He tutted. "And what is she?"

I paused, trying to work out the best way to respond. "Demigod," I answered eventually. The skinny man looked up at me over the rim of his glasses, disdainfully.

"I can see that, she'd already be dead otherwise. How strong? Will she be able to handle Ambrosia?"

"I, erm..." Anger rippled through me as I struggled to answer his question. Look at me! One of the twelve most revered beings in the damned world and a tiny human was looking at me like I was an idiot.

"She is powerful," I said eventually. But I had no idea if she could withstand Ambrosia. It sent those without enough power completely mad, and was highly addictive to those on the cusp. But it healed mortal wounds so it was a risk worth taking if required.

"Fine. I'll try something else first, but if it does not work, it will have to be Ambrosia. You can pay, I assume?" His eyes flicked to my headband as he spoke.

"Of course I can," I snapped. "Get on with it." He gave me a sarcastic bow.

"Voithos!" he barked, and a sprite appeared from a

minuscule doorway in the back of the room. She was only two feet tall, and moved as fast as a cat.

"Yes, Giatros," she squeaked.

"Get me some epikóllisi, and hurry up."

"Of course," she said, and scampered off to the shelves. I watched absently as sheer wings popped out of her back, and she hovered up the shelves, scanning for whatever she'd been asked to find. Giatros had fetched a large stone bowl and was pounding an orange flower in it.

If the girl died now, could I find the demon without her power? The days after Zeus had left, when I'd had nothing, were some of the darkest of my extremely long life. What was the God of War without strength? My father had stolen the core of me, my essence, the thing that made me who I was. The thing that made the world both fear and love me. That made my subjects respect me, drove them to achieve great things.

If it hadn't been for that voice reminding me that my power existed in another form, in another world... I looked down at Bella, as Giatros smeared an orange paste onto her wound. The stuff made her skin look even more blue. The manticore toxins were spreading through her fast.

If she did survive, would she discover how she ended up in the mortal world to begin with? Did that damned cat know?

I looked around for Hera's spy, spotting her on the floor near to the stone table. Her gaze was fixed on the winged sprite as she flitted about the room, gathering bottles.

"Do you intend to pounce?" I asked her coldly.

She turned slowly to me, blinking. *"I have a vested interest in this girl's life. If she dies today, Hera will know that you are to blame."*

"Me? She got herself stung!"

"Because you goaded and distracted her."

"Why do you or your master care?"

"You know why, warrior god. And you had better pray that if she lives, she does not find out."

11

BELLA

Bright light penetrated my closed eyelids, and my first thought was that something furry had died in my mouth. Shit. I must have drunk too much tequila. I blinked, finding it hard to open my eyes, and a slight man with thick glasses hazily came into focus.

"What the..." Before I finished my croaky sentence, a rush of memories crashed through my brain. Joshua, dead on the ground. Ares, God of War, telling me I was a goddess. Hades, Persephone, Olympus... Escaped demons, huge cats with scorpion tails... "What happened?" I tried to sit up but my head swam and the dizziness stilled me.

"Drink this," the guy with glasses said, putting one hand behind my back and helping me to sit up. I did as I was told, recognizing the taste of nectar from when Persephone had given me some. Warmth and strength flowed through me as I sipped, and I concentrated on my surroundings. I was in a room lined with shelves on every wall, and it looked like a drugstore from a fantasy film. Glass bottles and stone bowls filled with crazy colored liquids and powders were everywhere. I jumped in surprise as a tiny woman with sheer pink wings appeared in front of my face, hovering excitedly.

"Erm..." I said.

"You got yourself stung by the manticore." My eyes snapped to Ares, standing a few feet from me, huge arms folded across his bare chest.

"What the fuck is a manticore?" The winged girl flinched at my cussing and I gave her an apologetic look. She gave me a hesitant smile and fluttered away.

"The cat with the scorpion tail," he said. I took another long sip as I tried to recall what had happened. We had been at the campsite with the fighters, and they had wanted me to be their cook. I replayed the scene in my head, until I reached the part where I'd tried to pull back on that tug in my stomach. Something had happened. I had felt something move through me, flow into my knife. But then... Pain. I guessed that was when the scorpion tail got me. Squashing the excitement that I may have actually used a little bit of magic, I looked at the thin man.

"Where are we?"

"My apothecary. I was able to heal you with epikóllisi paste, rather than using Ambrosia."

"What's Ambrosia?" The man's eyebrows shot up, and Ares coughed and moved toward me.

"Now that the poison is dealt with, we should get going," he said quickly. It appeared I'd put my foot in it again.

"Thank you for healing me," I said to the man. He shrugged.

"I do as I'm paid," he answered, but his eyes were warm and I didn't believe his indifference.

"Perhaps we should buy a few more things, while we're here," I said, turning back to Ares. "More of this paste seems like a good idea. I mean, we've only just started and I got hurt."

"You didn't just get hurt. You almost died," said Zeeva in my head. I gripped the edge of the stone table I was sitting on and peered down. Zeeva blinked back up at me, tail swishing.

"Was it that bad?" I asked her.

"You were blue, Bella. It was that bad."

"Then we should definitely buy more of that paste," I said, setting down my empty glass and pushing myself off the table. I felt surprisingly well for someone who had apparently nearly died. "Why don't I feel worse if I was so badly injured?"

"Your body expelled the poison very quickly, and the actual wound wasn't very deep."

"Oh. Good." I gave my body a mental high five for looking after me, then panic gripped me when I realized my knife was no longer in my pocket. As soon as I started frantically patting down my jeans though, Ares held out his open hand. My closed little knife looked tiny in his huge palm, and I snatched at it gratefully. "Thanks," I said, for some reason unable to meet his eyes now that he'd done something I was genuinely grateful for. His heavy shoulders lifted in a shrug, and I realized that avoiding his eyes meant I was staring straight at his nipples. Heat flushed through my cheeks.

"I know how it feels to lose a weapon," he mumbled.

"Right," I said awkwardly, and spun to the storekeeper. "So how about some more stuff that'll save my ass again if I need it?"

We left ten minutes later, Ares grumbling about puny mortals and lighter drachma pouches, and my rucksack heavy with tubs of paste and bottles of nectar.

"Look, we don't know how close to one of these apothecary places we'll be if we run into trouble again," I said, then froze in my tracks as I stepped into the bright light and the sounds and smells of Erimos hit me.

We were in a bazaar, fabric-covered stalls surrounding us, and each filled with more delights than I could ever want. Food, weapons and clothes were on display everywhere I looked and my stomach growled as the smell of cooking meat washed over us. "Can we get something to eat?"

"Fine," he muttered, and stamped toward the nearest vendor. A large barbecue was set up across the front of her stall, and a joint of meat was spinning slowly on an iron pole over the smoldering coals. As Ares asked the woman behind it for two portions, I ambled over to the next stall. It was selling armor, but nothing like Ares' gleaming, clanky gold stuff. This was all soft, supple leather, and it looked badass. I wondered as I stroked my fingers down a leather corset top if the manticore stinger would have had more trouble penetrating my skin if I'd been wearing something like this. The t-shirt I had been wearing was torn and bloodstained, and I'd had to change it in the tiny washroom in the apothecary.

"No," said Ares from behind me. I spun, and he held out a piece of meat on a small wooden skewer. I took it from him and clamped my mouth around it immediately. I was freaking ravenous.

"No, what?" I asked him, once I'd swallowed a few mouthfuls.

"No clothes shopping."

"But if I had armor I might not have been hurt," I protested.

"I am not wearing armor," he said, gesturing to his ridiculously perfect chest. "And I was not hurt."

"No, but you seem to be happy using my magic power as a shield whenever you damned feel like it," I snapped back. He glared at me for a few seconds, then tossed his empty hand in the air in annoyance.

"Fine. Buy yourself some armor. You'll still end up dead in a damned day."

"Ooh, first time I've heard you use a naughty word," I said, grinning and holding out my hand. He shoved the rest of his meat, minus the skewer, into his mouth, then pulled the drachma pouch from his pocket and dropped it moodily into my hand.

"Damned doesn't count as a swear word," he muttered as I pulled the corset from where it was hanging.

"It does where I come from."

"You're a long way from home, Enyo."

"My name is Bella," I corrected him. And as I stared past him at the thriving, angry city, I couldn't help the feeling that the rest of his statement was wrong too.

After the stallholder enthusiastically demonstrated the magically reinforced quality of the leather armor by stabbing it repeatedly with a sharp knife, and allayed my concerns about the corset's lack of upper coverage by producing wide shoulder straps that laced into the bodice, I was sold. It was awesome. I wanted to put it straight on, but Ares grumbled something about finding a caravanserai for accommodation and gossip, and stamped off before I had time to unlace it.

"I think we should talk about what happened," I said as I skipped along beside him, trying to keep up as I rammed my new leather-wear into my bag. It was too big, and I eventually gave up, draping it over my arm instead as we weaved through the crowd.

"You are angry with me that you were injured? It was your own fault."

"Why would I be mad with you that I was injured? I was the one careless enough to get stabbed," I said. "I'm mad with you because whenever you use my power it throws off my focus. And that's what makes me good. My focus. I need it. I can't have you messing it up every two minutes."

Ares let out a long sigh. "It is called war-sight. Not focus."

"What?"

"Everything slowing down and you being able to anticipate other's moves and block out distractions. It is called war-sight."

I frowned up at him. I'd relied on those abilities to keep me alive countless times over the years, and it was weird as hell hearing someone else describe them. "So, it's part of the war magic?"

"Yes."

"And I've been using it in the normal world all these years?"

"A small part of it, yes."

"When I got that burst of tingly energy, was that me using a large part of it?"

"Yes."

"Why did it go into my flick-knife?"

Ares slowed, finally turning to look at me. "We will not discuss this here," he said. "There is a child stealing from you."

"What!" I whirled, tearing my rucksack away from a skinny, shirtless kid who yelped in surprise. "Fuck off and steal someone else's shit!" He looked down at the bit of fabric in his hand that he'd managed to pull from the bag at the same time I did. My panties. He was clutching a pair of my damned panties. "Give those back!" But he was off, racing through the crowd like a whippet. Before I could tear off after him, Ares gripped my shoulder.

"We do not have time for this."

"He stole my godamned underwear!" I spun to Ares, outraged, and for a moment I swear I saw the corner of his mouth quirk up. But his words carried no hint of humor at all.

"Then I regret not informing you of his presence sooner."

"You knew he was trying to rob me and you said nothing?"

"You were being annoying."

"I was asking questions I need answers to!"

"You were being annoying," he repeated.

I bared my teeth at him. "You know, I'd almost forgotten that you were a giant asshole." Dark embers danced through his eyes, and I realized that insulting him when he didn't have his helmet and armor on was quite different than before. I could see the muscles twitch in his jaw, the skin across his forehead and eyes tighten, his hair move against his shoulders as he swelled and tensed. His anger resonated in me, the excitement and challenge of it intoxicating.

"Do not call me an asshole," he ground out.

"Or what?"

"Or-" he started, but I never found out what my alternative was. At that exact moment, the two us were lifted clean off our feet.

12

BELLA

"That's them," barked a voice, as I kicked and flailed my feet as I spun in the air. The minotaur from the fighters' camp came into view as I twirled uselessly, an armored guard next to him holding a tall staff that glowed.

"Put me down right now!" roared Ares.

"You're coming with me," the guard answered from under a purple fabric helmet. He turned and began to march through the courtyard, people moving out of his way with sideways glances, and I began to bob through the air behind him. The minotaur gave me a vicious smile as we passed her.

"How are we floating?" I ground out, as I bounced against Ares' enormous arm. A spark of electricity zipped between us and he scowled as his hair fell over his shoulder.

"The staff. All the guards have them. They encase people."

"Right. How do we get out of being encased?"

"We don't. They're designed to restrain people in a world inhabited by the strongest and most violent fighters in existence."

I gritted my teeth, panic beginning to coil in my stomach. I didn't do well with being trapped. Not since my stint in prison. "I assume they can't hold gods?" I asked, angrily.

"Of course not. But you do not have the power of a full god, and therefore neither do I."

I balled my fists as I drifted too far from Ares to hear him, and a small creature that I guessed was a satyr walked underneath me. He was a little two-legged goat, his bearded face the only human-looking thing about him. Nobody seemed surprised or concerned to see us floating through the bazaar after the guard. It must be a common occurrence in Erimos. When I drifted close to Ares again, I spoke. "Where is he taking us?"

"Hopefully not to the King," he muttered. My arm bumped against his again, and more sparks fired. "Is that the staff's magic?"

Ares just grunted. I glanced down at the ground, wondering where Zeeva was, but I couldn't spot her. I wasn't sure if that was good or bad.

Energy was coursing through me with nowhere to go, and I knew I needed to calm it, to slow my panic. I took a long breath, flexed my fingers, and patted the pocket with my knife in it. Enjoy the scenery, I told myself. Learn about where you are. When you're in a situation you can't control, make a list.

. . .

After ten minutes of being bounced through the air of Erimos, my 'things that will help me survive in the city' list didn't have much on it. There seemed to be an endless array of creatures living in Erimos. Beautiful women were everywhere, some with skin that looked like water, others with skin that looked like tree-bark. Muscular human men mingled with creatures that appeared to be made up of the most bizarre animal combinations imaginable. Many had wings and tails, and all looked like they could take a punch or two.

The guard marched on without pause, so I was only afforded fleeting glimpses. We were heading toward the center of the city and the buildings around us were becoming more opulent as we went. There were no more noisy bazaars, but the shady doorways we passed were definitely selling trade. Several appeared to be drinking establishments, men and women stumbling in and out, clutching goblets. More were brothels, I was guessing from the number of scantily clad bodies leaning against the jewel-encrusted building-fronts. And they were certainly not all women. This place looked to be a pervert's dream, I thought as I stared wide-eyed at a four foot tall creature with six arms, and six breasts. She gave me a little finger wave as I passed, and I mutely returned the gesture.

The next part of the city we passed through felt different again. The buildings were taller, and a number of them reminded me of churches or temples, bulbous spires over grand arched doorways inviting folk in. It was clear the guard wasn't heading for any of these though. The enormous central tower that dominated the view above us was clearly our final destination.

Eventually we slowed, and as I turned gently in the air, I tipped my head back and gazed upward. The tower was massive. It glittered and gleamed with colored gems in the bright light, and the curved main body of the structure was adorned all over with intricate carvings of weapons. Small arched windows were cut out of the stone in a curving spiral and I couldn't help my burning curiosity about what was inside.

We floated over a shining blue walkway, which morphed into grand steps leading up to an even grander doorway. Columns that mimicked the shape of the tower lined our path, and as we entered the magnificent building, my breath caught.

We had floated into an oasis. In the middle of the huge round room was a pool, the most luscious and inviting turquoise color. Around it were daybeds draped in soft white fabric, and vividly green palm trees offering their inhabitants privacy. I could hear birds calling as we carried on down the blue walkway toward the pool, and the jewel-encrusted walls were giving off light high above us, dappled and soft. Three or four naked women were in the water that I could see, and waif-like girls scuttled between the daybeds carrying trays of drink and small bowls.

The guard stopped abruptly, dropping to one knee, and Ares and I bumped against each other again as our invisible tether to the staff went slack.

"I have the man you asked for, my Lord."

I felt Ares stiffen before we drifted apart again.

"Are we about to meet the King?" I hissed.

"You are indeed," boomed a voice, and the palm trees fluttered as a figure stood up from the largest daybed. I felt my mouth open in surprise when instead of walking around the pool to us, he stepped onto the surface of the water, barely leaving a ripple where his feet met the liquid.

He was tall, slender and gorgeous. If Aladdin aged as well as George Clooney, this man would be the result. His black hair was thick and full, and he was wearing long purple robes, tied loosely at the waist and exposing most of his chest. Row upon row of gold bands hung around his neck, and there were too many pendants for me to make out what they all were. As he reached our side of the pool I could see his face properly, and my heart began to hammer in my chest the second our eyes made contact.

Something about this man was wrong. I knew it as surely as I knew my own name; I could see it in his dark eyes as though it were tattooed on his forehead.

The man flicked his hand, and whatever was holding us in the air vanished. I failed to get both feet steady under me as we dropped to the floor, and my pride burned as I stumbled onto my knees. After so long off the ground, both my feet were tingling and numb. I leaped back up, hoping my cheeks weren't giving away my anger that I had fallen, but the man's gaze was fixed on Ares.

"Well, well, well," he said, a cruel smile crossing his handsome face. "I never thought I'd see the day."

"Hello. I'm Bella," I said, loudly. His eyes flicked to

mine. My heart pounded in my chest, my pulse racing. I would not look weak in front of this man. I would go on the offensive early. Establish myself as strong.

"I know who you are."

"I doubt that," I answered. "But I have no fucking clue who you are. Help a girl out?"

His eyes narrowed and he cocked his head at me.

"He is the King of Erimos," said Ares. His voice was loaded with pent-up anger, and my own energy responded instantly, fizzing through me.

"Now, now," the King said smoothly. "I'm a little bit more than that. As you well know," he smiled at Ares. "I am one of the three Lords of War," he said, looking back to me. "Appointed by the great god, Ares." My heart skipped a beat. "Pain, Panic and Terror. Together we walk in the mighty god's wake, basking in his deadly power." He spread his hands as he spoke, then looked slowly back to Ares. "That is to say, when he *had* power."

Shit.

My stomach dropped as I looked at Ares. It seemed that taking his helmet off hadn't made him as invisible as he'd hoped it would.

13

BELLA

"**A**s your ruler, you must bow to me," snarled Ares. The King stared back into Ares' furious face.

"Make me," he hissed. I felt the tug in my stomach at the same time the King cried out, doubling over into a painful looking bow.

"Do not play games with me, Pain," Ares said.

Pain? My head whirred as I tried to piece information together. The King had said there were three Lords of War; Pain, Panic and Terror. And Ares had just called him Pain? But he was so beautiful...

"So the rumors are not entirely true," the King croaked as he straightened. "You have some power remaining."

"Has an Underworld demon passed through Erimos in recent weeks?" barked Ares, ignoring the statement.

"Yes," Pain answered.

"Really?" I couldn't help my excited response, and

the King looked at me. His gaze bore into mine, and I instantly regretted showing my enthusiasm.

"Why do you seek this demon? Are you are here on Hades' bidding?"

"Why we are here is none of your business. Tell me where the demon went," Ares said.

"Was he alone?" I added quickly.

"You assume this demon is a *he*?" Pain smiled at me, and an uneasy feeling rippled down my spine. That smile held a malice that I didn't possess. I was filled with anger and energy and a desire to physically feel the world around me, but I did not yearn for pain, nor to inflict it. This man however... It oozed from him.

"Answer the damned question!" shouted Ares, and Pain whirled to him.

"You are in my domain now, holy one, and your little show of power only served to confirm that you are indeed weak," he hissed, the tower darkening around us. "My brothers will be here momentarily, and we shall decide together what to do with our once mighty leader. Until then I suggest you take a seat." I felt movement behind me and glanced back to see two large wooden chairs appearing out of nowhere. I had my knife in my hand, though I had no recollection of taking it from my pocket, and my racing pulse was causing blood to pound in my ears.

"*Bella, listen to me.*" Zeeva's voice in my head almost startled me into dropping my weapon. "*This is Ares' fight. It is Ares' realm, his subjects, and his pride you face. If you want to find your friend, you must let him lead this.*"

Every instinct in my body ached to throw myself at

creepy, hot Aladdin. But her words rang so clear in my head they drowned out my other thoughts.

This was Ares' fight.

I looked at the two men, Ares refusing to sit down and an epic stare-off in progress. She was right. I would be pissed if someone stole an important fight from me.

I slowly put my knife back in my pocket. I wanted to ask Zeeva where she was, but I couldn't mind-speak like she could. I remembered her saying that I had to project my thoughts to her and folded my arms across my chest. With a pointed sigh, I sat down hard on the seat behind me. Both men broke eye-contact with each other to flick glances at me. I gave them a sarcastic smile.

"Don't mind me," I said. "Please, continue eye-fucking one another." Ares bared his teeth, but they went back to staring at each other.

"*Where are you?*" I thought the question as hard as I could whilst holding an image of my stuck-up cat in my head.

"*By the closest palm,*" came a reply a moment later. Giving myself a mental high-five for managing to make contact, I scanned the pool fast, and saw a tiny flicker of a tail behind the nearest tropical tree.

"*How'd you get in here?*"

"*I followed you. People do not notice small cats here. Listen to me. The Lords of War are powerful, each able to inflict the power they embody with so much as a look or a word. Do not goad Ares whilst in the presence of the Lords. It is extremely important that they do not realize his volatility. Do you understand me?*"

"*Gods, you sound like my old teachers,*" I answered, rolling my eyes.

"*Bella, do you understand me?*" she repeated, her mental voice hard.

"*Yes!*"

"*Good.*"

The air before me began to shimmer, interrupting us, and with a flash of red two more men appeared. Two men who could not have looked more different from one another.

One was a similar stature to Pain, tall and slender, but instead of being dressed like an Arabian sultan, this guy was dressed like Robin Hood. He was wearing leafy green breeches, had a white linen shirt on that was also open to his navel, and tall leather boots. Sandy colored hair curled over his ears, and when he looked at me his green eyes shone with something just as dark and unsettling as I saw in Pain's eyes. The third man... The third man was so striking that once I started looking at him, I couldn't stop. He had no features at all. He was a humanoid mass of something solid; smooth and hard and mesmerizing. Whatever he was made of was covered in a marbling effect, black and white swirling and moving and blending over what I guessed was his skin. His blank face fixed first on me, then on Ares.

"My Lord," a hissing voice issued from him, like nails dragged down a blackboard. It made my skin crawl.

"Terror," responded Ares stiffly, before turning to

the Robin Hood guy. "Panic," he acknowledged just as curtly.

So, these were Ares' three Lords of War. I resisted the urge to stand up and introduce myself. I was going to do exactly what Zeeva had told me to do. For once in my life, I was going to behave myself. Avoid trouble. Not be a dick.

"Now you are a delectable little surprise," said Panic, turning to me. "Where have you been hiding?" I bit down on my lip to stop myself responding.

"Aw, she's shy," hissed Terror. "Maybe we can find a way to liven her up." Fear shot through me, his innocuous words laced with a threat I never, ever wanted to see fulfilled.

"Maybe you can find a way to back the fuck up," I said, leaping to my feet and whipping out my knife. The two men with faces smiled.

"I see she is perfectly susceptible to our power," Terror said. I clung to the words as my heart hammered. He was called Terror. He embodied fear. I wasn't really scared of him, he was just using magic. I repeated the sentence in my head, drawing on it to calm the fear.

"I'm sure you're perfectly susceptible to my foot up your ass," I said, parroting him.

"Bella!" Zeeva's voice hissed through my head. Shit, I was supposed to be keeping my mouth shut. This was Ares' show. I sat back down as Terror cocked his head at me. The black and white swirled and swished across him, like black oil over a marble statue.

"Delectable was a good choice of word, brother," he said quietly. Another stab of fear gripped me, and I bit down too hard on my lip this time, tasting blood. Pain let out a long, satisfied breath, his eyes widening as they focused on my mouth.

For the first time in my life, I did not want to be at the heart of the action. I very badly wanted to be anywhere but where I was. I wasn't used to feeling afraid, or out of my depth, or weak. But power oozed from these three men, and it was dark and foreboding and just plain fucked up.

"You are here to tell me about the Underworld demon who is hiding in my realm," said Ares loudly, and all three Lords looked at him.

"I must say, you're rather dashing under all that armor," Panic said to him. "Who'd have thought the God of War would be so pretty?"

Ares was hot as hell, but not pretty. The word had been used to rile him. But I felt no tell-tale pull in my gut, the indication that Ares was getting mad and using my power.

"Tell me about the demon," he demanded.

"The trouble is, we don't take orders from anyone weaker than we are. Nobody in this realm does," Terror said slowly. "That's the way you designed it. He who is strongest, rules. And by all accounts, you are no longer the strongest."

Ares stepped forward, but not rashly or angrily. Deliberately. I felt my pulse quicken. "I am the son of Zeus, God of War, one of the twelve Olympians and most revered beings in existence," he said, and thrills shuddered through me at the tone of his voice. When he wasn't stamping around like an overgrown toddler, he was freaking *fierce*. "Make your decision carefully, my Lords. For I am eternal, and you only exist within my realm and my power."

I could see the doubt cross the faces of Pain and Panic, fleeting but real.

"There is nothing in this realm that cannot be won in a fair fight," said Terror eventually. He was clearly the ringleader of this little trio. "We know of the demon you seek. We know of their plan, and who they are working for."

I opened my mouth, but Zeeva hissed loudly inside my skull and I closed it again.

"Prove that you are still our true leader. Pass a trial that each of us set for you, and demonstrate your dominion over Pain, Panic and Terror."

"You will regret this," the God of War growled.

"We are only living by the standard you have set," said Pain, bowing low. Oceanus's words came back to me, about Ares earning his power back by being a true ruler within his own realm.

"If you can pass the tests, then we will hand over your demon. All wrapped up with a bow," grinned Panic.

Ares stared at him, then pointed at me. "The girl doesn't leave my side." Terror's statuesque form turned to me, and I gave him the finger.

"Fine," Terror said.

"Excellent!" exclaimed Panic, clapping his hands

together. "As we're already here in Erimos, would you like to start us off with your trial first, Pain?"

"It would be my pleasure," the Lord grinned. "I've got just the thing.

"I believe something so heroic should not go unwatched," said Terror, moving his hand to his featureless face thoughtfully. "We shall host a feast tonight, in honor of these..." He paused. "Ares Trials. Yes, I like that. Then you may embark upon Pain's test tomorrow."

"There will be no feast," growled Ares.

"Oh, but there will, mighty one," Terror said. His voice was harsh and sing-song at the same time, and I hated it. "Or we won't allow you to take the girl with you. And we both know that would be a serious blow to your chances."

Did Terror know who I was? And that Ares only had power around me? Or did he just think I was important to Ares somehow?

Either way, we didn't have time to screw around at feasts. "What about the demon and the people he's kidnapped? We don't have time for feasts," I said, standing up. Not one of the four men looked at me. I heard Zeeva sigh in my head. "Can you at least give us some proof that you do really know where the demon is?" I tried. The thought of being this close to finding out if Joshua was OK and being forced to wait uselessly was more than I could handle.

"Are you questioning our integrity?" asked Pain, looking at me.

"Well, based on what I have learned so far, yeah.

You all seem like a bunch of twisted jerks," I said. "I get bad vibes from the lot of you."

Pains lips curved up into a smile. "Few insult the Lords of War so freely, and without repercussion," he said. A stabbing pain started in the bottom of my skull, and although I stopped myself making a sound, I couldn't help the flinch of my face. Slowly the pain moved down my neck, my muscles tensing and warping as my nerves reacted.

"Stop. Her request is fair. You are all dishonest." Ares voice was loud and hard, and mercifully, the pain stopped. I took a deep breath and straightened my body, sweat beading on my forehead and chest. Fury was simmering inside me, my instinctive reaction to pain. The desire to destroy things burned through my blood, and my gaze fixed on Pain as red shrouded my vision. Hot older Aladdin or not, this guy was going to get a kick in the balls the first opportunity I got.

"Fine. Once you are satisfied, I shall summon the guests and we shall see you back here in two hours." Terror waved his hand, and a huge iron dish on a stand appeared before him. Gently flickering orange flames danced in the center, and they suddenly flared white and bright.

An image materialized over the dish, amongst the white flames. A hooded creature was reaching out, touching the face of a woman laid out on a dark stone slab. She didn't look dead, her skin was a healthy color and her mouth moved as she breathed. But she didn't react when a blackened claw raked over her cheek, leaving the faintest red mark. My stomach twisted into knots as I stared.

There were rows and rows of slabs surrounding her, all with bodies stretched out on them. And directly to her left, looking for all the world like he was in a restful sleep, was Joshua.

"Joshua! Take us there, now!"

"Calm down, little girl. All in good time." Fury stormed inside me, fear for Joshua, outrage that this had happened to him, guilt that I had spent a single moment since getting here not thinking about him, was all building into an uncontainable rage within me.

"He doesn't have time! Look at him!"

"I don't know who 'he' is," said Terror, waving his hand and the image in the flame dish vanishing, "but I can assure you that the demon's plans are not immediate."

"What is it? And who is it working for?" Ares barked the questions as fury and fear pounded through me. Normally I would have hurled myself at someone by now, but these three... Their power was enough that my instincts were frozen. I knew that they would tear me apart before I moved a foot.

But that didn't stop me wanting to.

I would find a way to make them pay. Once I'd rescued Joshua, I would find a way.

"You have not earned those answers yet, mighty one. We have made a deal. Complete the Ares Trials, and we will hand the demon over. See you in two hours."

~

We were escorted roughly from the tower, and I barely saw the people or stone around me for the red haze. "Don't fucking touch me!" I bellowed at a guard as he tugged at my elbow once we were out of the grand doorway. He jumped backward, then scowled and strode away.

"We need to-" began Ares, but now that I was no longer in the presence of the Lords, the need to hit something was too great to restrain. With a roar, I smashed my fist into the nearest wall, the bite of pain as my knuckle split on the sharp gems only spurring me on. Before I could land another punch, there was a bright flash, and I froze, heart crashing against my ribs as I looked about. We were back at what was left of Ares' pile of rocks. Where we had started.

"Go ahead," he said, and sat back on his heels, just as I had done when he had gone apeshit with his sword. I blinked at him, then with a roar, booted the pile of rocks as hard as I could with my steel-capped boots. Over and over I kicked at the boulders, unbridled rage brimming up and flowing out of me as the rocks flew and smashed beneath my feet.

Eventually, exhausted, I fell back on my ass, rubbing my hands across my face hard enough to hurt.

"They know where he is, and they won't tell us," I said hoarsely. I felt utterly powerless. Frustration was the worst feeling in the world. "They could end this right now, but I can't do a thing."

"Nothing comes for free in Olympus."

"All those people though!" I turned on the ground, looking at Ares. "They're just letting all those people be held captive, so that they can play games with you?" Ares said nothing. "That's fucked up! Do you understand how fucked up that is?"

"When the great gods were allocated power, many shared the parts of it they didn't want with others," said Ares quietly. "Some power is too great and complex to be wielded by one. For example, Athena has the power of war strategy, a refined version of what I..." He paused, then corrected himself. "We have. Which is the rawest form of the power of War. Anger, glory, valiance, courage, strength." I stared at him, trying to work out what he was telling me. "But War is about much more than valor. War involves Pain, and Panic, and Terror. War involves Death and Violence and Discord."

"So, those powers all live in different beings?"

"Yes. My sister is the Goddess of Chaos and Discord. Keres demons, who reside in the Underworld, are the spirits of violent death. They swarm over battlefields, feasting on the souls of those most brutally killed." A shudder rippled through me. "And the Lords of War... They are directly of my creation. They are of my power."

I shook my head. "No. No, you don't feel like them. *I* don't feel like them, and you said we share the same power."

"You do not understand," Ares said, and pushed himself to his feet.

"No, you're right. I don't." I stood too. "Explain it to me."

He let out a long sigh. "All you must know is that your friend is in no imminent danger, and that the Lords cannot be blamed for their behavior. They exist purely to behave as they do. And they are necessary."

"It's necessary for your world to have twisted assholes in charge?"

Ares raised one eyebrow in an uncharacteristic quirk. "Olympus would not be Olympus without twisted assholes in charge," he muttered.

I could feel my anger dissipating fast, hard resolve replacing it. If those pricks were telling the truth about the demon, then Ares was right, and Joshua wasn't in any immediate danger. And at least I now knew he was still alive. Nobody in the image over the dish looked like they were in pain, messed up as all the stone beds were.

And now we had some sort of plan. If we completed these Ares Trials, we would get him back, and capture the demon. As fucked up as it was to play with people like this, I needed to accept that we were in a better position than we had been before we entered Erimos.

"You just swore," I said to Ares.

"Hmmm."

"Do we have to walk back to the city now?"

"Yes."

"Will you tell me how to use my power on the way?"

"No."

As we began trudging back to Erimos, I thought about what Ares had said. He said the Lords of War were 'directly of his creation'. Did that mean he had literally created them? Or fathered them perhaps? Or just that his godliness came with a side of Pain, Panic and Terror?

I considered asking him, but I had too many other things to straighten out in my head first, and this was probably the only stretch of silence I would have for a while. I had to adjust my game-plan. I was no longer on a demon hunt with the God of War. I was now partaking in three Trials designed to defeat him. Maybe kill him. Could he even die?

I had a lot to add to my 'questions to ask later' list, I realized. Like why was my useless cat so keen that I didn't land Ares in trouble when the Lords showed up? In fact, why was she with us at all? I still had no idea. A bolt of worry for her moved through my chest, and I hoped she had made it out of Pain's tower safely. The fact that she had been my only pet, and company, in London was impossible to shift, despite her disinclination to tell me anything helpful. Although my many evenings spent stroking her did seem pretty weird now.

I looked up at Ares' muscular back, his shoulders flexing as his arms swung, his tied ponytail moving against tanned skin. Why am I attracted to a miserable, humorless brute? I should add that to the list of questions.

If I was being honest though, I was lacking evidence that he actually was a brute. My initial impression of him, dressed in armor and wielding a sword over the bleeding body of my only friend, may not have been entirely representative. So far, even when I'd deliberately annoyed him to the point of lashing out, he hadn't hurt me at all. And as far as I was aware, he'd given up on his notion of wanting to kill me for my power pretty quickly.

He *was* miserable and humorless though. And he was using my power and not telling me how to. Which meant he was definitely still an asshole. Just not quite as asshole as these new assholes.

I let out a sigh, and he turned his head to me as he walked.

"You are tired already?"

"Fuck no," I retorted. "I was just lamenting there being so many assholes in the world."

"Why do you swear so much? I dislike it."

"I swear so much for exactly that reason. People like you, who think they can dominate me, dislike it. Plus, there are many situations in life where only a creative swearword will do."

"Like what?"

"Well, there was an old homeless man in London I once heard call someone a wankwaffle for throwing a sandwich at him. I thought that was an excellent use of creative swearing."

"Wankwaffle?" The word sounded so ridiculous

coming out of Ares' mouth that within seconds my small chuckle had turned into full on laughter.

"Say that again," I gasped, through cackles, and to my sheer delight, he did. Hysterics took me completely, tears streaming from my eyes as my brain replayed the mountain of seriousness before me saying the word *wankwaffle*, over and over.

"You are very strange," Ares said eventually, when I'd recovered myself enough to resume walking beside him.

"I needed that," I breathed, my cheeks aching slightly.

"You needed to hear me saying wankwaffle?"

A snort of fresh laughter escaped me, and I reached out and punched him in the arm. "Stop saying it! You'll set me off laughing again!"

"I do not understand how you can be furious and fearful for your friend one moment, and laughing hysterically another," he said, shaking his head.

"I think it has to do with being so overwhelmed that it's either laugh or drink all the tequila and cry," I told him.

"Tequila makes you cry?"

"Sometimes," I admitted. Though I had never shed a tear in front of another person. Not since my first foster family. I mean, tears of laughter or pain notwithstanding. I'd been in many fights that had caused my eyes to water. But never tears of sadness.

"Then why do you drink it?" I looked up at the huge god, the bewilderment on his stunning face obvious.

"To escape."

"Escape what?"

"Boredom, mostly."

The confusion cleared from his expression as he glanced down at me. "Your mortal world is extremely boring," he said with a nod.

"Yeah," I said. And now I had a chance to live where I truly belonged, and never be bored again. I just had to work out how to use magic.

15

ARES

I usually enjoyed feasts in my own realm, thrown in my honor. Especially when the other Olympians attended, and they could see the deference my subjects gave me first-hand. But this was not one of those feasts. Aphrodite attending was the only upside I could see to the entire circus.

She looked even more stunning than usual, if such a thing was possible. Today her skin was dark and rich, and her hair a pale blue, in masses of curls that framed her soft face. I longed to run my hand down her cheek, to run my fingers down her throat, to feel her stomach tense beneath my touch as I moved lower. But she had been seated at the other end of the long table in Pain's dining hall when we had eaten, and since the gathering had been moved to the opulent oasis, she had not yet approached me. My pride still stung from her dismissal of me the last time I had seen her. I would not look weak by going to her first, like a keen puppy.

So, I stood still by a large palm tree, with my arms folded across my armored chest, and glared at everyone who walked near me. It felt good to have my helmet back on. Really good.

"Brother."

I barely moved my head an inch, to see my sister, Eris, sauntering toward me. "Must you wear such revealing clothing?" I asked her.

"Yes. It upsets, delights and confuses people in equal measure. Besides, they're naked." She gestured at four mer-women, swimming seductively in some sort of dance in the clear water of the pool. Many guests were watching them appreciatively, including Pain.

"I see you haven't killed the girl yet." Eris said.

"Of course I haven't," I grunted.

"And is that because Hades forbade it, or because she's so pretty?" She smiled at me and took a long sip of her drink.

"Keep your mouth shut, sister."

"Not one of my strengths," she said, mock apologetically. "And if I did, I wouldn't be able to tell you what I came over here to tell you."

I let out a long breath. "Fine. What did you come to tell me?"

"I know what Zeus is doing with your stolen power," she whispered, her eyes shining.

Every muscle in my body froze, her words spinning through my head. Zeus was using my power?

"What?"

"Did you think he just stole it just for fun?"

"He stole it to stop me defeating him," I growled. Eris pouted and tilted her head to one side.

"Oh, little brother, you can't defeat daddy, even with your power. He's far, far more powerful than all of us. Silly boy."

Anger rumbled through my gut, and I only just stopped myself reaching for Bella's power. There was no point alerting her to this conversation. I looked automatically across the pool, to where she was having an animated conversation with the same severe white centaur who had been at Hades' ceremony. Well, Bella was having an animated conversation. The centaur was barely moving as the girl threw her hands around as she talked excitedly.

"What is Zeus using my power for?" I ground out instead, looking back at Eris. There was a very good chance she was lying. My sister was not known for her honesty.

"Come now, I'm not going to just tell you! Where's the fun in that?"

"This is not a game!"

"Actually, thanks to your lovely Lords of War, that's exactly what it is now. You know, I was going to put my drachma on her dying in the second Trial, but now I'm not so sure. There's something about her..."

Curiosity flashed in her eyes, under the casual tone. She was desperate to know more about Bella.

"She is human. She will likely die in the first Trial," I snapped.

"She may be mostly human now, but I'm not stupid,

or weak, Ares." Eris' tone had changed, no longer play-ful. "There's power under the mortal layers. And if she sheds those and reaches it, she could be strong." I said nothing, and she continued to stare at me. "She told me, Ares," she said eventually. "She told me that she is the Goddess of War. That's what you're using her for, isn't it?" Still, I said nothing, staring out over the pool. "But there is no Goddess of War. There never has been. So, I'm left wondering, however did you find her?"

"Leave me be, Eris," I said, unfolding my arms and looking at her. "I have business to attend to." Before she could respond, I strode away from her, looking like I knew exactly where I was going. The truth was though, I just needed to be away from her. My sister was one of the most shrewd and dangerous women in Olympus. And I knew what she would say next. She would offer me more information about Zeus and my power, in return for information about Bella. Information that was too valuable for me to give up, even if the thought of someone else using *my* power burned a hole in my insides. It wasn't like me accessing Bella's power, because that was the same magic. It was a part of both of us. But using a god's power that had not been prop-erly allocated to you?

It was a gross violation of everything deities held close. And Zeus, whilst wrong in his most recent actions, was our immortal leader. There was no way he would stoop so low. She was lying.

"I told you that your Lords might have some revenge planned," cooed a voice. I felt my pulse leap as I whirled around.

"Aphrodite," I said, giving her a curt nod, that belied my racing heart.

"Are you worried about the Trials?" My eyes were drawn to her full lips as she spoke, and desire washed through me. She lifted a long-stemmed glass to her mouth, the movement slow and impossibly sexy.

"Stop it," I said. She rolled her eyes at me, but the fierce need to touch her lessened. "Of course I am not worried about the Trials. I created the Lords. Anything they design will be to my strengths."

"Has it occurred to you that that means they know your weaknesses too?" She raised one perfect eyebrow as she looked at me and I faltered before answering her.

"No. They are driven by valor as much as anyone else in my realm. Their tests will show off their power."

"And your first one is Pain? That should be fun to watch." Her beautiful eyes sparkled.

"Would my pain arouse you?" I asked her quietly.

"Not explicitly, no. But I long to see the beast in you again. And maybe a dose of pain will bring it out."

I clenched my teeth. I longed to feel the beast in me again. But there was nothing there but hollow rage. "I will have my power back soon."

"And you expect me to wait for you?"

"I expect nothing from you." That was a lie. As long as I could remember, I had expected things from the woman who dominated my thoughts day and night. And she had never, ever fulfilled any of them outside of lust.

"Good." Her usually warm voice was clipped and cold, her soft beauty hardening before me. The Goddess of Love was not all sugar-sweet whispers and sensuous caresses. Love was one of the most cruel things in the world, and Aphrodite embodied it all. But the side of her that was attracted to a man like me was rarely on display in public, and true-to-form, a beaming smile replaced her hard look as Pain approached us.

"Lord Pain," she said, as he reached her. He took her hand and bowed low as he kissed it.

"Oh, divine goddess, you are a vision," he said smoothly. She gave him an appreciative nod.

"Your brothers are here tonight?"

"Indeed." He turned and pointed to where Terror was sitting in a large chair, a tree-dryad girl on his lap and an Erimosian girl dancing before him.

"Tell me, what is it that he is made of?" Aphrodite asked curiously.

"Marble." Her eyes darkened, and jealousy fired through me instantly. I knew that look well.

"So hard to touch... I wonder..." she whispered, and Pain's smile spread slowly wider.

"An audience with the goddess of love would be an honor for the Lords of War," he said. "All three of us would be at your disposal, day or night."

"Now, there's an idea," she said, voice like sweet honey.

The need to lash out gripped me, almost intolerable, and as Pain's eyes flicked to mine, malice dancing in them, I turned away. For the second time that evening, I strode across the tiled floor with faked purpose, needing to be anywhere else.

The goddess toyed with me as though I were a plaything. An image of her laying naked on her bed, the three Lords around her, aroused and hungry, filled my head and a hissing snarl escaped my mouth. I changed direction, heading for the large doors of the tower. I did not care if Pain had the satisfaction of causing me to leave my own feast. I was done for the night.

16

BELLA

"Oh dear. The goddess of love has upset my brother. Again." Eris gulped down more of her drink as I watched Ares storm out of the tower doors.

"Are they friends?" I asked, as casually as I could.

"Why? You interested?"

I gave a slightly too loud snort. "Hell no. I mean, he's hot. Like really hot. But so is everyone here." Too much delicious fizzy wine had followed too much delicious rich food, and I was feeling dangerously talkative.

Joshua. Lords of War. Manipulative goddesses with massive boobs. Remember what's at stake. Keep it together, Bella.

"Well that's true. Folk are either gorgeous or half wild-animal in Olympus. Although I suppose some men are a bit of both." She waggled her eyebrows at me and I laughed.

I knew I shouldn't, but a large part of me couldn't

help liking the Goddess of Chaos. I mean, I wouldn't tell her my secrets, but I'd sure as hell party with her.

"Do you have a partner?" I asked her.

"Many."

"Oh."

"One of the perks of being immortal."

"I'd have thought that would make it harder to find love," I said.

"Love? Gods, I thought you were less naive than that, sweetie," she exclaimed. "Love is a concept best left to those less... volatile. And anyway, it's dull."

"How can you find anything in a world like this dull?" I asked her. She gave me a long look.

"Sweetie, I thrive on discord. Shit going wrong. Look around you. With Hades and Poseidon in charge and 'Oceanus the long-lost Titan' playing nice, there's not a lot for me to do. Zeus fucking things up for a while was excellent, but now he's gone. You, and these new Ares Trials are the most exciting thing to have happened around here in a while."

"Well, I can't wait to see the rest of Olympus," I said, draining what was left in my glass. When I looked back at Eris, she had a strange, almost pitying look on her face.

"I'm starting to hope you get the chance," she said eventually. "Tell me about your world, where you grew up."

"Sorry, I'd better follow armor-boy," I said. "He may be a giant asshole, but we're kinda bound to each other until this is over."

"He'll just be sulking in his room; stay and have another drink."

I eyed her, her smile too wide, her eyes too narrow. I wasn't drunk enough or stupid enough to trust her, no matter how much I liked her company. "Thanks, but no. See you later."

Before we had left for the feast, my bag and new leather armor had been left in a plush room in a small but grand tower I was informed was called a caravanserai. Basically a Erimosian hotel. As I stepped out of the tower to make my way back there, I saw that the bright sunlight had disappeared completely, and although I could see no actual moon above me, a cold blue light that could easily be assumed as moonlight glinted off the embedded gems in the buildings around me. The streets were busier now than they had been earlier, many more young men and women leaning against walls of buildings, offering 'exotic delights' or 'magnificent returns' or 'wild rides'. The buildings I had assumed to be drinking establishments earlier had humans and creatures alike streaming in and out of them, some looking elated, more looking desperate. I channeled my best 'back the fuck up, I'm a badass even though I'm not dressed like one' energy. Everyone I was passing was armed, and all either wore clothing appropriate for a desert, or barely anything at all.

"Well if you don't have it by this time tomorrow, we'll have to find another way for you to pay," snarled a voice from the darkness between two buildings on my right. There was a loud slapping sound, and a gurgled shout. I forced myself to carry on. I wasn't there to meddle in other's business.

But the knowledge of an impending fight called to me, and my feet slowed of their own accord. Someone screamed, shrill and loud, and a man's laugh accompanied it.

I stopped walking.

"This is no business of yours, little girl," rumbled a voice far too close to me, and I leaped to the side, away from it. Something stepped out from the shadows at the end of the alleyway.

"How did I not see you there?" I breathed, staring. It was only a little taller than me, but had massive leathery wings that were torn and covered in spikes. Its body was leathery too, with a small piece of fabric hanging from a belt to cover its genitals, and it had legs that looked more like a bird's than a human's. But my eyes were drawn back to its mostly human face. It was as though half of it had been melted, all the features on the right-hand side a good inch lower than those on the left. Tufts of thin hair stuck out over its skull and I couldn't have told you the thing's gender if my life had depended on it.

"It's my job to blend in." I felt my eyebrows rise. How could a creature like this blend in to anything? I heard a thump from behind him in the alley and another scream, this one muffled.

"What's going on back there?" I asked. Energy was swirling through my middle, building fast.

"None of your fucking business."

True. But not good enough.

"So, do you just guard alleys while someone else does the beating?"

"The boss only hits on folk who don't pay," the thing grunted. So, this thing was a mob-heavy. This really wasn't any of my business. Maybe I should just walk on.

"You can go and screw yourself, you fucking bully! I'd rather you killed me than took everything away from her," I heard a voice in the alleyway cry.

They were giving themselves up to defend someone else. A lover, a wife, a child? Either way, my interest was piqued. From those words I knew that this person had courage and honor. Another thumping sound echoed from the alley, along with another cry.

Red slowly descended over my vision. I cocked my head at the thing in front of me. "Move."

The thing just snorted, its lopsided mouth quirking into a smile. I shrugged, then darted forward, dropping into a crouch and hitting out hard with my fist. I caught it exactly where I wanted to, right in the muscle in the side of its thigh, and it gave a small shout as its leg crumpled beneath it. Before its knees had hit the ground I was back up, kicking out hard and catching it under the jaw, which was now waist-height. There was a sickening crunch, then the thing's eyes rolled back into its head and it tipped slowly backward, unconscious.

I turned and strode into the alley. As I got further into the gloom I could see a large man, shirtless and tanned, dark hair slicked back from his hard face, pinning a boy against the rough wall.

"Hi," I said, and the older guy's head snapped to me.

"Grothia?" he called loudly.

"If that's wing-thing back there, they're gonna need some medical attention," I said. The boy's eyes widened as the guy's narrowed.

"This is none of your business. Leave."

"I can't," I said, with another shrug. "You're right, this has nothing to do with me, but I can't help feeling that your punishment of this young man exceeds his crimes."

"You think you're some sort of vigilante?" he said, a cruel smile spreading across his face. "It's been some time since we've had one of those in Erimos."

"Put him down," I said. I was painfully aware that not twenty-four hours ago I had been holding Joshua against a wall in the same position. My guilt morphed into anger, more strength pulsing through me.

Slowly, the guy slid the kid down the wall, and the boy's own hands went to his throat as soon as he let go. One side of his face had a long red line running down it, and I immediately looked for the blade that must have caused it. Sure enough, the glint of metal shone in the guy's left hand as he turned fully to me.

"You don't look like you're from around here, little girl," he said. "So I'm going to give you a chance to turn around, and walk away."

I squinted past him, to see if the kid could escape down the other end of the alleyway while I distracted the jerk, but it was too dark for me to see. The boy stayed where he was, hand on his throat. Oh well. I'd have to knock the goon out then, same as I had with wing-thing. "No, thank you," I said, and slid my flick-blade from my pocket.

"That's a little knife," he said, holding his own up and twirling it, showing off its size. It was curved, like a scimitar.

"Little knife for a little girl," I answered, and threw it at him.

He didn't move fast enough, and it sank into the top of his shoulder as he yelled. The kid sprang to his feet, but before I could feel any sort of relief for his escape, he launched himself at the mob-boss.

"Wait!" I started, then froze as I realized what he was doing. He yanked my knife from where it was deep in the guy's flesh, avoiding the wild stabbings from the scimitar in the wailing man's other hand. The kid moved fast, and my stomach lurched as he threw me a backwards glance, then ran.

"Shit!" I raced after him, ducking under the useless swipe from the bleeding mob-boss, and powering after the kid. There was no fucking way I was losing that knife. "Come back, you ungrateful little thief!" I bellowed, as he flew out of the other end of the alley, which I could now regretfully see was not a dead-end after all.

He banked sharply to the left, and I pivoted on the balls of my booted feet, chasing after him. There were more people on the streets here, colored lanterns casting soft light over the glittering walls, and the smells of meat wafting through the air. We were moving toward the bazaars.

I followed the kid through more twisting, turning streets, until we burst into one of the wide courtyards filled with fabric-covered stalls. Panic rushed through me as I took in the sheer number of people and places to hide. If I didn't catch up to him soon, I would lose him - and my knife - for good.

"I saved your damned life, you shit!" I hollered, forcing more energy into my legs, turning up my speed. How was he so damned quick? Not many people could outrun me. The idea of losing my weapon, the only thing I'd managed to hold onto my whole life, the thing that had saved me countless times, was making anger build inside me, and my vision darker.

My eyes locked on the kid as he slowed down, reaching a three-way crossways between stalls. I watched as his body began to shift, his weight moving from one side to the other, and made a desperate guess at which way he was about to turn. I banked fast to my right, praying he was going to do the same. I could cut him off.

With a surge of speed I flew around the stall, and just as I'd hoped, he barreled straight into me, his head turned to search for me behind him. I swiped at his neck as he stumbled backwards, and he cried out as I gripped him. That familiar bolt of guilt ripped through me as I noticed the already red marks from the mob-boss' fingers around his throat, but the red mist blocked it out.

"Give me my fucking knife back, now!" I roared, as I

lifted him up. He was taller than me, but my grip was iron, and his feet scrabbled on the ground as he beat at my hand with his. "I can keep this up all night, kid. Give me back my property." When purple began to tinge his face, he finally reached into his hareem pants pocket, and pulled out my flick-blade. I held out my other hand and he dropped it into my palm. I let go instantly. "I was trying to help you, and you stole from me. What gives?"

"I don't need your help," he croaked, backing away from me. eyes red.

"It kinda looked like you did, kid."

"He was right. You're not from round here," he spat, then turned and raced away, into the crowd. I cocked my head after him. This place really was full of tough people.

No vigilantes required.

And still no friends for me.

"*I'm pleased you recovered your knife without killing anyone.*" Zeeva's voice sounded in my head and I scanned the ground for her, spotting her prowling from behind a stall selling meat skewers.

"Why would I kill someone?" I answered her, shoving the flick-blade possessively into my pocket. "And why was he such a shit?"

"*Even those with good in their hearts are different in the realm of war.*"

"Huh. Well, I'm glad you're here. I have no idea where I am."

17

BELLA

All the way back to the caravanserai I asked Zeeva questions, and all her answers were vague and unhelpful.

"As I told you, the longer you are in Olympus, the more of your power will be accessible to you. I am guessing being in this violent place may speed things up." I could hear the distaste in her voice, and wondered briefly what Hera's realm was like compared to this one. But I dismissed the question in favor of more useful ones.

"If I get more power will I still be human?"

"Right now you would be termed a weak demigod. Mostly human, with some divine power. The stronger you get, the higher class demigod you will become. I do not know if it is possible for you to lose enough of your humanity to become a full goddess."

"But if I started out as the Goddess of War, with the same power as one of the twelve Olympians, how the hell did I become human?"

Zeeva didn't answer me for a long time, silently

stalking through the busy streets. *"The story of your origin is not mine to tell. And I could not tell it fully, even if I wanted to."*

"The story of my origin?" I repeated, glaring down at her. "You make me sound like a fucking super-hero." Despite being accused of being a vigilante once already that day, I couldn't see myself wearing a cape and fighting crime.

Perhaps super-villain would be more fun.

"You are no hero, Bella. But you could be something. Something more than you could ever have been in the mortal world."

"I know," I said quietly. And I did know. I knew it to my core. I was meant to be here. I belonged in a world where even the good guys were dicks.

When I finally reached the place I was staying I was still buzzing with energy. A woman with tree-bark skin was standing in a grand hall hung with luxurious burgundy and gold fabrics and an enormous staircase stretching up the center of it. The woman smiled when I told her who I was, and gave me a small orb that shone ruby red. I followed her up the impressive staircase and was sure that we must be at the top by the time she stopped and pointed to a door. A small round hole in the center of it glowed red, and I looked at the orb in my hand, then at the tree-woman. She nodded at me, leaf green hair falling over her shoulders. Hesitantly, I pushed the orb into the hole and there was a little click, and the stone door swung open. The red orb popped suddenly back into my hand.

"Huh," I said. "Thanks. Do you know which room my friend is in?"

She nodded mutely at the door next to mine, then turned and made her way back down the stairs.

I knew Ares wouldn't want to see me. But I had questions for him, both about my power, and about whatever it was we would be doing the next day. So instead of entering my room, I strode to his door, and knocked loudly.

"No!" came the immediate shout.

"I need to talk to you," I said through the door. There was silence, followed by a thud, and then the door opened abruptly.

"The terms will be set out by Pain tomorrow. There is nothing I can tell you now."

"Erm, I was kidding when I said about you sleeping in the helmet," I frowned, staring up at his gleaming gold-covered head. I squashed an urge to reach up and flick the red plume.

"I just put it back on to talk to you," he grunted defensively.

"Why? I spent all day with you without it."

He glared at me through his eye slits, peering closely. "You have too much energy. Why?"

"How do you know how much energy I have?"

"You are swaying and bouncing and flushed."

"Oh. I tried to save a kid from getting beaten up by a mob-boss and a really ugly thing with wings, and he stole my knife."

"Who stole your knife?"

"The kid."

He shrugged after a short pause. "You were careless to let it get stolen."

"He stole it from where it was embedded in the mob-boss' shoulder!" I protested. Ares let out a long sigh, then stepped to the side, holding the door open.

I gave him an over-the-top grin and stepped into his room. It was one hell of a room. I'd never been to Morocco, but I'd drooled over plenty of five star hotels on the internet, and this was exactly what I had seen pictured. Soft, dim light came from painted glass set in the stone walls, which were draped with deep, rich yellow and red fabrics. A dresser, large closet and enormous bed were all made from wood so dark it was almost black, and the cushions on the mattress shone like they were made from real gold.

"Nice room," I whistled. There was a clanking noise behind me, and I turned to see Ares lifting his helmet from his head. All the pent-up energy in the world couldn't stop my body from momentarily freezing, as my pulse rocketed.

There was something so sexy about his face being revealed, something so beautiful about his hair falling over the metal chestplate of his armor. Something so strong and fierce and just freaking hot about all of him.

"What is a mob-boss?" he said, snapping me out of it.

"Erm, a gangster."

"What?"

"You know, lends people money, knowing they can't

afford to pay it back. Then blackmails them and beats them up."

"A gambling hall owner?"

"That would fit, yeah."

"There are many in Erimos. Which one did you kill?"

"Woah now, armor-boy. I didn't kill anyone."

He almost looked disappointed as he frowned at me. "Then why are you here?"

"Because I have questions for you. I want to be able to use my power."

"No. Leave."

"You can't just march about using my power and not letting me have any of it!" I threw my ass down on the bed, to make a point that I wasn't going anywhere. Ares pinched the bridge of his nose, and I took the opportunity to examine his lips. They were freaking excellent lips.

"I should not have let you in here. I thought you needed my help with the guards because you had killed someone."

"I don't kill people. To be honest, I'm not thrilled that it sounds like you do."

"I am over three thousand years old, and the God of War. How is it you thought I would not be responsible for some death during my life?" There was a grit to his voice that was obviously meant to intimidate me, but, as seemed to be the case with his anger, it just fired me up more.

"I guess when you put it like that, it's not really your fault," I shrugged.

"You belittle my achievements? Say they are not really my fault?" He stared at me, muscles twitching under his gold armor.

"Look, I get that you have to do a certain amount of nasty stuff, it's your job. But I wouldn't call killing people an achievement."

"What if the person I am killing is a tyrant? A murderer? A threat?"

We were back to that vigilante idea again, I thought, pondering his words. Did anyone ever deserve to be killed? "We all deserve a second chance," I said eventually.

"You are mistaken," he snorted. "Many here deserve nothing but death."

"Here in Olympus, or here in your realm?"

"Both. Leave me now."

"But you need to tell me how to use my power before tomorrow. If you distract me again like you did today at the camp we could fail Pain's Trial."

"All you need to do is stay out of the way, and I will win."

"Look, armor-boy," I said, standing up. "Do I strike you as the type of girl to 'stay out of the way'?" Ares said nothing, just glared at me. Gods help me, he was even hotter when he was angry. I shoved down the desire to see the fire in his eyes again. "I'm going to take your silence as a no. Pain is going to put us through something unpleasant at best, lethal at worst, and asking me to do nothing is unfair and quite frankly, not going to happen."

"Why are you making this so difficult?" Ares barked.

"Difficult? You are asking me to go against every instinct in my damned body!" I could swear when I said the word body his eyes flicked down my advancing torso. I jabbed my fist into his breastplate when I reached him. "You need me, and I need you. So, we work together or we both fail."

"No." He glared down at me. "I will repeat myself as long as I have to, irritating little human. I am over three thousand years old. I *created* Pain, Panic and Terror. With access to my power, their tests will be no match for me at all. If you want your friend back, do as you are told." He hissed the words, and I could see the burning orange starting deep in his eyes. A distant drum beat found my ears.

"Access to *your* power?" I repeated. "You mean *my* power!"

"Our power."

"My power! It's my damned power!" I shouted the words, the drums beating louder, and fire exploded in Ares' eyes. For a second the world around me vanished, the ring of steel sounding loud, a rush of adrenaline flooding through me as a blissful need for glory took me. Ares gripped my shoulders with both hands, pulling me into him, and heat ripped through my core as something fiery and fierce and untamable burned in his expression.

But with as much force as he'd pulled me to him, he pushed me away, taking a huge breath.

"You will leave now."

"Not until you tell me how to use my power." I half choked the words, drums and steel and heat and fire clouding my mind. And a rare throbbing between my legs that radiated through the rest of my body, fueling the powerful energy and throwing me completely.

He moved to the door, swinging it open hard and avoiding looking into my eyes. Was he feeling this too? "Get out."

I did as he said, not because he had told me to but because I didn't trust myself with him a moment more. When he'd pulled me to him... I'd wanted him to kiss me. What the fuck was I doing wanting him to kiss me?

"This isn't over." I managed to fling the words over my shoulder as I stormed out, hoping to hell he thought I was talking about the argument about my power and not the fact that I apparently had the hots for a three thousand year old giant asshole warrior god.

18

BELLA

I hadn't realized how tired I was until I threw myself down on my own equally plush bed. My eyelids drooped as I stared at the cloth-covered ceiling above me, my churning brain and fired up body slowing down fast.

I'd never had a problem falling asleep. Except when I was in solitary confinement. But that wasn't emotional, that was physical. I had so little to do, so little to vent on, so few ways to expend energy in that fucking awful place that I didn't need to sleep.

Today, I needed to sleep. Perhaps it was my war magic at play all this time, making sure my body got what it needed to be a good fighter. I thought about the laser focus that I now knew was actually called 'war-sight', and yawned. I forced myself to sit up and pulled my shirt off over my head, then reached down to untie my boots. Sleeping in boots was not cool.

A flash of curiosity whipped through me about what Ares wore to bed, and I rolled my eyes.

Joshua. Think about Joshua. You're going to save him from whatever the fuck that rotten-handed demon was, kick his ass for lying to you, then see if he wants to be your boyfriend, I told myself firmly.

My jeans soon followed my boots onto the floor and I tipped backwards again, letting out a sigh as I hit the mattress. Where had all this sexy stuff in my head come from? I rarely thought about sex at all, writing it off as something I could only do with guys who meant nothing because they all bolted when they found out what I was really like.

That's not to say I didn't enjoy it. But I'd never understood why people went so nuts for it. My admittedly fairly limited experiences had left me pent-up and hyper, craving something I couldn't get. I had to assume that I either wasn't doing it right, or I hadn't found the right person. Someone caring and patient like Joshua might be the exact sort of lover I needed to get me to wherever it was I couldn't reach.

Someone hot and fierce and untamable could get you there a hell of a lot quicker, my confrontational inner voice quipped. I shoved it down. Maybe I was hormonal. Maybe it was avoidance. I probably shouldn't underestimate the psychological impact of being told you're a goddess and being kidnapped to a fantasy world.

Yes, that was probably it. Ares had turned my world upside down and awakened a possibility that I didn't have to live the life I hated anymore. And my overwhelmed brain was confusing my excitement about everything I had yet to discover about magic and

Olympus with him. Joshua would call it 'projecting' in our sessions. I was projecting my burning desire for a new life in a world where I belonged onto Ares, in a different form of burning desire.

I pulled the thin silk sheet over myself as I nodded. That was definitely it. And now I knew that, I could ignore it completely, and concentrate on getting through the Trials and saving Joshua.

But it wasn't Joshua's eyes that burned with promise in my mind as I drifted off to sleep.

Waking up in the softly lit Moroccan-looking room took me so much by surprise the next day that I was sitting bolt-upright, searching for my knife before I had even blinked the sleep from my eyes. The events of the last - I didn't even know how many hours - tumbled through my head as I stared around at the beautiful room.

I was once the Goddess of War. I was meant to be like this. I finally had a reason for all the fuck-upery in my life. And there was power inside me that could make me even better.

Guilt doused out the excitement rippling through me as the awful image of that blackened hand on the girl's face came to me, Joshua laid on the stone table beyond. This wasn't about me. Once Ares had his own stupid power back I would be free to learn how to use mine, and then I could get excited. But first, I had to save my friend.

Guilt-driven determination settled over me as I swung my legs out of bed. If Ares was going to refuse to let me use my own power, I would have to find a way of working with him that wouldn't get me killed, like it almost had at the fighters' camp. I pulled on my jeans and unzipped my bag, looking for a t-shirt.

"It would be a shame not to wear that leather armor you were so excited about," said a lazy female voice. This time I didn't jump in surprise. I was starting to get used to Zeeva showing up in my head uninvited. Plus, she was right about the armor. I'd clean forgotten.

"Morning, Zeeva."

"It's in the closet over here." I looked around for her, finding her sitting in front of one of two large dark-wood closets.

"Thanks," I said. "Am I supposed to wear something underneath it?"

"That's up to you."

I thought about it as I opened the closet wide. There were dresses in there. Lots of very pretty, brightly colored flowing dresses, covered in sparkling jewels. I paused, cocking my head at them. I literally couldn't remember the last time I had worn a dress. With a small shake of my head, I pushed them along the rail until I came to the brown leather corset.

It took me a full ten minutes to work out how the many metal catches and thick leather cords could be adjusted, but eventually I had the thing on. I stood in front of the mirror that lined the inside of the closet door and moved experimentally, watching as a massive grin overtook my face.

I looked like I felt, for the first time in my life.

My black skintight jeans were more like leggings anyway and moved with me, but my top half... The wide straps that had been added to the corset made it feel secure as well as protecting my shoulders along with my ribs and other important organs. I had chosen to wear nothing underneath the armor because the body of it came high enough that I wasn't at Eris levels of cleavage, but it still made me feel... well, sexy as fuck. The material lining the inside was intensely soft, not rubbing or moving at all as I bent over and stretched, testing it.

"I look badass, right?" I asked Zeeva.

The cat flicked her tail. "Yes," she said. My eyebrows shot up. I had expected her to mock me.

"Really? You really think so?"

"Yes. You are beginning to look as you are supposed to look."

"I knew it!"

What would Ares think of it? The question was in my head before I could help it, and I replaced it quickly with, what would Joshua think of it? Probably that it would encourage my violent psyche, I thought with a frown. I gave a small shrug and closed the closet. My violent psyche might just be what saved his life, if I could survive Ares' Trials.

A loud bang on my door told me that I was about to find out what Ares thought, whether I wanted to or not.

"We must leave," his gruff voice hummed through

the heavy wooden door. I grabbed my knife off the nightstand, pushing it into my pocket, and opened the door. The God of War stood huge and hulking before me, armor and helmet in place.

"Good morning to you too," I told him, turning back into the room. He stayed put just outside the door as I grabbed my boots, pulling them on. "Do we leave all our stuff here?" I asked him. He nodded, his red plume bouncing. "I see you're talkative as ever today," I muttered, as I tied my laces.

"You are hoping for an apology?" he said.

"No. But if you've changed your mind about not letting me use my own power being dangerous then-"

He cut me off. "Hurry up, or we will be late."

"Late for what?"

"The Trial announcement."

Panic fired through me, not at the imminent news of our fate, but at something much more alarming. "I haven't eaten yet!"

Ares let out a long breath. We'd been together five minutes, and the sighing had already begun.

"We will get something on the way."

He got me more of the tasty meat skewers from a stall as we made our way through the stone streets toward Pain's tower, and I tore into one as soon as he passed them to me. Now that he was in full armor, gleaming and gold, many people in the streets were staring at him. The hawker hadn't even charged him for the food.

"I have a question," I said, around a mouthful of

delicious greasy meat. He didn't say anything, so I carried on. "Is the reason I can always sleep and eat, no matter how upset or in danger I am, part of my power?"

"Yes," he grunted. "You need to be battle-ready, always."

"I thought so! It makes so much sense now. I just thought I was a bit heartless."

"You were likely that too, until you became human." I looked sideways at him.

"And how did I become human?" I asked the question as casually as I possibly could, but his eyes darted to mine and there was nothing at all casual about them.

"I don't know." I scowled, and shoved more meat in my mouth.

"What is this?" I held up my last skewer.

"I don't know."

"You know nothing, Jon Snow," I quoted, shaking my head and eating more.

"My name is not Jon Snow. You are irritating and confusing," Ares said tightly.

I sighed. "At least I have a sense of humor, armor-boy."

"I have plenty of humor."

"Really? Tell me a joke."

"I do not know any jokes."

"You shock me," I replied sarcastically. "What do you find funny then?"

"Many things."

"Like what?"

"People falling over." I looked up at him, licking my fingers.

"I should judge you for that, but to be honest there are whole TV shows of people falling over to laugh at where I'm from."

"TV shows?"

"Yeah. Plays shown on screens you can watch from anywhere."

"You mean a flame dish?"

"What?"

"A flame dish. Like the one the Lords used to show us the demon."

So those flame dishes were the Olympian equivalent of a TV? I thought about that a moment, throwing a glare at a scruffy kid whose eyes lingered on me too long. There was no way I was getting robbed again. The streets of Erimos had already cost me a pair of panties and almost my knife.

"Can you see anything you like in these dishes?" I asked Ares.

"Gods can use them to broadcast images, and they can be used to communicate with one another. But they are rare, only the wealthy and powerful have them."

"Huh. What do you think Pain's Trial is going to be?"

"Gods, do you ever stop asking questions?" he groaned.

"In my defense, I have been here one day. There is a lot to learn."

"Find someone else to ask. Like that insolent cat." Zeeva, as usual, was nowhere to be seen.

"But how would she know what your Lord of War

would be thinking? Do you think whatever it is will be painful?"

"Given that he embodies pain, yes," he answered, slowly, as though I was stupid.

It was a fairly stupid question, I supposed. Of course it would be painful. I mean, I wasn't scared of pain, but I certainly didn't crave it, or get off on it. In fact, I would go pretty far to avoid it. Anticipatory nerves tingled through me and I changed the subject. "Do you like your sister?"

Ares gave a loud bark of annoyance, throwing his hands in the air. "Be quiet! I am trying to mentally prepare myself for battle and you will not shut your mouth!"

"I talk when I'm nervous," I said.

"You are the most irritating being I have ever met! I should have just killed you in that damned human building, before that cursed cat showed up!"

The memory that accompanied his words, of the shock of finding Joshua and then seeing him towering over the body, sent me instantly from nervous-energy-mode to pissed-off-mode. I felt the skin on my face tighten, and my hands ball into fists.

"You couldn't kill me if you wanted to," I snarled. Ares said nothing, but his pace increased. My much shorter legs couldn't keep up with him without skipping, and he knew it. More anger fizzled through me. "Without my power, you're just a big muscular brute, and nothing more. I bet I'm faster than you."

"Pray that you never find out which of us is the

better fighter," he hissed, whirling on me suddenly. I squared my shoulders, glaring up at him, but his eyes flashed inside his helmet, and he spun back, marching off down the street again. I gave him as vicious a finger flip as I could manage, and then stormed after him.

19

BELLA

Pain's tower looked just as it had the last time we had entered it, he and his creepy brothers standing in front of the oasis, a huge flame dish between them. Servants lined the entrance, all shapes and sizes, and all dressed in purple robes.

Ares didn't pause as he strode toward the Lords. I was annoyed that I was trailing slightly behind him, so I put on my best 'couldn't-give-a-flying-fuck' face and slowed down instead, so that I didn't look like I was chasing after him. I glanced about myself like I owned the place and tried to ignore the unpleasant feeling tingling through me. I knew that if I looked over, Terror's featureless face would be trained on me. I could feel it.

"Let's get on with this outrage," snapped Ares, and I was forced to look at him and the Lords.

Pain wore a smile from ear to ear, and Panic winked at me. My lip curled up, and something dark flashed through his eyes.

"Good day to you, mighty Ares," said Pain, giving him a slow bow. "Are you ready to face the worst of your realm?"

"Get on with it!"

"As you wish."

There was a blinding white flash, and we were no longer in the tower. I could hear sound before I could see anything, the brightness from the flash replaced with harsh sunlight. As the world came back into focus around me, my jaw hung open.

The sound was hundreds of people cheering and shouting, from row upon row of stone seats, ringing a massive sandy stage.

We were at the top of a gladiator pit.

"You intend to make me fight in the pits?" snorted Ares. "You set me no challenge at all." He sounded cocky and sure of himself, as I continued to blink around. We were in a high box, lined with soft fabric and comfortable looking chairs, that overlooked the whole pit. The crowd were mostly human, but there were plenty of creatures I could make out in the crowd who had wings, or fur, or animal limbs. I swear I could see one person with her hair on fire.

"This is a particularly special fight," Pain smiled. "Hence the excellent spectator turn-out." He gestured to our right, and I turned to see another well-furnished box, occupied by a figure made of smoke, and a beautiful white-haired woman. Hades and Persephone. She gave me an encouraging smile and a finger wave. I dumbly held up my hand in response, but my fingers didn't move.

I'd fought in rings back home most of my life. I fought for money, for glory, to tame an un-scratchable itch. But this...

This was no dark and dingy basement with shitty boxing ropes marking the boundaries. This was no stinking, cheaply-made aluminum cage, surrounded by bellowing drunks that made a grab for my sweaty ass every time I left a fight victorious.

This was the real fucking deal.

I gaped down at the sandy stage in the middle of the ring. Though far away, I could see dark smears that were surely blood. Iron bars blocked five or six gates surrounding the stage, and I wondered what they kept behind them, below the stepped rows of benches. Animals? Warriors? Monsters?

"Good day, Olympus!" called Pain, and his voice was somehow amplified, filling the huge space. Everyone in the crowd fell instantly silent. "Welcome to a rare spectacle indeed. Your warrior God, Ares, is here today to prove his strength to us all." He paused to throw a smile at Ares. "And he will be fighting with a human companion!" Mutters rumbled through the assembled folk. I shifted my weight, a hand going instinctively to my knife for comfort. "There will be three rounds, two today, and a finale tomorrow, provided they live that long."

Ares gave a small hiss as laughter and louder chatter rippled through the fighting pit.

"As a divine God of your stature, we need to put you at a disadvantage of some sort," said Pain, and Ares stiffened. Was Pain not going to acknowledge the fact that a god with no magic powers was already at a freaking disadvantage? Did the crowd know Ares had no power? "You may either wear your armor into the ring, or take your sword."

"I will not fight without either," growled Ares. I felt a small tug in my gut, and even though his size didn't change, he seemed to loom larger in the box. Terror's stone face turned my way, and my skin crawled instantly.

He knew. I was sure he knew that Ares was using my power. Instead of asking about fucking flame dishes, or arguing about using my power, I should have been asking more about the Lords, more about what the rest of Olympus knew about Ares' loss of power. Frustration filled me as I realized how woefully under-informed I was.

"Then you forfeit," said Pain with a shrug, snapping my attention off Terror.

"Never."

"Then choose. Armor or Sword."

I knew which he would choose, even before Ares yanked his sword from its sheath. I couldn't see his eyes, but I could feel the fury rolling from him.

"You will regret this," he said through clenched teeth, before crouching and laying his weapon on the carpeted floor. I saw that same flicker of doubt that I had seen the day before cross Pain's face, but Terror spoke.

"So you keep telling us," he said lazily. "We are acting exactly as you have trained us to act, mighty one."

Ares straightened, and I felt a sudden jerk in my stomach. A tiny crack appeared down the side of Terror's face, and he took a step backwards, a sharp intake of breath escaping his stone exterior.

"I want to begin now," said Ares, and with a sideways glance at Terror, Pain clapped his hands and we flashed again.

"What the fuck did you do that for?" I hissed, as soon as the second flash cleared and I saw that we were now standing in the middle of the sandy ring. I walked slowly in a small circle, looking up at the now roaring crowd surrounding us.

"He needed to be reminded of his place," said Ares, his voice still loaded with fury.

"Save it for the Trial!" I pointed at the crowd. "Do they all know that Zeus stole your power?"

"No. Absolutely not. Hades and Poseidon have forbidden all knowledge of Zeus' actions to be public."

"Well, your Lords worked it out pretty quickly. I reckon your rumor mill is pretty busy," I muttered. "What are you going to do without a sword?"

"The same as you," he grunted.

"I have a knife," I said, pulling it from my pocket and flicking it open.

"I have these," Ares said, and smashed his fists together, making the armor over his forearms ring loudly.

My instinct to compare him to the Incredible Hulk died on my lips, as his eyes sparked. He *was* pretty impressive, if I was being honest.

And his strength and anger was doing something to me. My usual adrenaline hit before a fight felt like it had been multiplied by ten, delicious energy coursing through my body, making it hard to stand still. My eyes were flicking between each of the barred gates around us, and slowly everything before me became tinged with red. I was ready.

A booming rumble began, and the sand-covered stone beneath my feet began to move. Large jagged bits of rock began jutting up from the ground and I looked fast between them, noticing metal shining in all of them.

"Are they... swords? Like actual swords in stones?" I called over the noise.

Ares moved toward the closest one as the rumbling stopped. "Yes."

"Mighty Ares! This will be your only chance to procure yourself a weapon! If you cannot remove the weapon from the stone, you shall continue the competition unarmed!"

"What about me?" I protested, and Ares flashed me a look.

"I thought you had a weapon," he said snarkily, then pulled himself up the nearest rock. It was about five feet high and uneven, but he made short work of getting to the shining sword hilt buried in the top. A deep scraping sound made my head snap to the left, and I saw one of the iron gates barring the doors into the ring start to lift.

"Ares, something is coming," I called, as another scrape followed it, and a second gate lifted.

One by one they all started to rise, and I looked back to the warrior God as he closed his hand around the hilt of the sword and screamed.

I could actually see the electricity around him, it was so intense. Purple and yellow sparks of power leaped and danced across his metal armor, and he tipped his head back as he wrenched his hand from the weapon.

"Careful now!" sang Pain's voice across the pit. The crowd roared with laughter.

It's a test of pain, I reminded myself, as Ares stared down with burning eyes at the sword. And this god would back down from nothing, of that I was sure.

I couldn't help flinching as he moved again, closing his fist for the second time around the sword hilt. This time his scream was more of a groan, but just as much sparking electricity bounced over his body.

The sword moved though. Only an inch before Ares let go again, chest heaving, but it did move.

I looked warily back at the open gates. If Ares didn't get the sword out before whatever it was we were supposed to fight came out, then I might just have to show him how much he had underestimated me.

20

BELLA

As Ares pulled on the sword for the third time, a figure stepped out of the gate on my left. Heart pounding in my chest, I turned to face it. Taller than Ares by a few feet, the thing had one gleaming blue eye in the center of a flat face, shrouded in a deep hood. The cape dropped all the way down its body but was open enough for me to see that it was wearing a small white wraparound garment held over its thighs by a leather belt. In one hand was clutched a tall staff, sparking with the same energy that was tearing through Ares from the sword.

In time with a yell from the God of War, the staff stopped glowing. I looked between the two fast. The staff had stopped glowing when Ares had let go of the sword.

They were connected. The staff was the source of the electricity, I was sure.

"We need to destroy his staff, then you can get the sword!" I shouted.

"I will get the sword myself," Ares barked, and lunged for the hilt again. I screwed my face up as two more cyclopes stepped out of two more gates, each with glowing staffs. Shit.

"You're an idiot! Let's deal with these guys first, then getting the sword will be easy!"

Ares let go of the sword with a snarl, his chest heaving even harder than before. "I will get the sword, pain or none!" he roared.

"Pig-headed fucking moron," I snapped, not quite loud enough for him to hear, and turned back to the nearest enemy. I would bet all the drachma in the world that I could disable all these one-eyed bastards before he could get that stupid sword out of the rock.

Challenge set for myself, I ran at the first cyclops.

It was like hitting a brick fucking wall. I smashed my fist into its chest as I launched myself at him, but instead of him reacting, or my fist sinking into flesh, I bounced backward five feet. The damned thing didn't even look at me. I staggered backward, stumbling as I tried to stop myself falling, and my bruised pride caused more anger and strength to surge through me.

"You're getting it this time, asswipe," I hissed through clenched teeth. Taking a bigger run up, I tried again, but instead of going for the cyclops, I made a grab for the staff as I reached him.

This time he did react. Fast. His single blue eye locked on me, and he moved, swinging the staff out of my reach and bringing it swiping toward my legs. But my focus, or war-sight, had kicked in, and I saw his muscles move, his body shift, the momentum of his actions, all before the actual event. I knew exactly what was coming. I jumped early, clearing the staff and coming back down just in time to land on the metal, bringing the thing crashing to the ground. The cyclops let out a hiss as instead of letting go of the staff, his body followed. He tumbled onto the sand, and I moved fast. With as much strength as I could muster, I brought my boot down on the glowing end of the staff.

I heard the scream rip from my mouth, but it didn't sound like me. Agony was tearing through my body, every nerve ending on fire, every sense totally over-loaded, as electricity coursed through me. With a mammoth effort, I threw myself back, breaking the contact, and the pain abated instantly. Sweat rolled down my back and my forehead, as I panted for breath. The cyclops was struggling back to its feet, lifting the staff high, as Ares shouted again. I looked dizzily at him as he gripped the sword up on the rock. Now that I knew how fucking awful the shocks were, I couldn't believe that he was still up there. The sword had only moved another inch or so.

I looked back at the cyclops, trying to think of another way to rid him of his staff, and paused. He was staring in dismay at the end of his staff, which was no longer glowing. It was no longer doing anything at all.

I'd broken it. My big fucking boots had broken it! Giving myself a mental high-five and the cyclops a sarcastic grin, I raced towards the next one. He didn't follow me, just dropped the useless staff to the sandy floor and folded his arms. Weird. But definitely not a bad thing.

To my relief it looked like only three of the creatures had come out of the six gates. I wasn't sure I couldn't handle another one of those shocks, let alone six of the fuckers.

"Why aren't you guys fighting us?" I asked the second cyclops loudly, as I neared him. His eye stayed trained on Ares, on top of the rock, just like the last one had. "I mean, you're helping me out with this whole statue thing you've got going on, but I'm a little suspicious," I said. The cyclops didn't react. "OK," I shrugged. "Your job is to guard the electricity staff thingy and nothing else. Fair enough."

With a lurch, I darted under the arm that was holding the staff, kicking out at the bottom of the long pole. He moved it out of my way in time, but in doing so leveled it out, so that it was parallel to the ground. After a split-second of apprehension about how much it was going to hurt, I grabbed at the glowing end, and yanked it with all my strength to the ground, forcing it hard onto the sand-covered stone. I faintly heard a smashing sound as pain engulfed me, then it was drowned out by the sound of my own blood pounding in my ears. I was on fire. I couldn't breathe. With a scream, I wrenched my arm away, moving my legs too, instinctively carrying myself farther from the vile staff. Thankfully the cyclops did exactly as the first had, dropping the other end of the now broken staff with a scowl and folding his muscled arms in front of him.

I swiped at the fresh wave of sweat rolling down the

back of my neck, my ears ringing. The only positive I could draw as I stumbled toward the last cyclops was that at least the shocks left no residual pain. They left me dazed and sweating and breathless, but once I broke contact, the agony stopped immediately.

"Are you ready to get your shitty staff smashed too?" I panted as I reached the third creature. I glanced back at Ares, as the cyclops ignored me. The sword was half way out now, and I was sure there was much less electricity sparking over him. Certainly he had stopped yelling. He must have been taking the shock powered by all three staffs, until I started destroying them.

I had just felt the shock from one each time, and that was bad enough. All three in one hit? I couldn't help the teensy bit of admiration that welled inside me. *He's an idiot for not just helping you,* I told myself. If he had, I wouldn't be about to get another one of these hurt-like-hell shocks.

But he hadn't helped me, so I was.

Dredging up more energy, I leaped high, kicking at the cyclops' hand that was holding the staff. He turned, moving it out of the way, but I saw the adjustment coming, and twisted in the air. A small shock gripped me as I made contact, and the cyclops actually made a grunting noise as the staff slid from his grip. I landed awkwardly, but rolled to the staff before the cyclops could scoop it up again, bringing the back of my heel slamming down on the glowing end.

Instead of the final shock I was expecting, I heard a roar of triumph from Ares, and no pain wracked my body at all.

"I told you I would get the sword!" the warrior God bellowed from behind me. But I didn't look at him. My gaze was fixed on the cyclops, just as his huge eye was on me. He was only a couple of feet away from where I was sitting on the ground, the smashed staff beneath my boot. He hadn't straightened and folded his arms like the others.

"Well done, little girl," the creature said, baring sharp teeth as he grinned at me. "Now those staffs are out of the way, we can play."

I barely rolled out of the way fast enough, his own massive boots crashing down where I had been sitting. I scrambled to my feet whilst still moving, seeing the other two creatures charging towards me on both sides. I darted for two lumps of rock, and heard a loud thud behind me. Pulling my knife from my pocket and flicking it open, I whirled.

Ares, gleaming and gold and magnificent, was wielding a fine silver sword and landing blow upon blow on the three cyclopes surrounding him. Indignation that the idiot man only had the damned sword because of me, but was now getting all the glory, swamped me, and I cried out as I charged into the melee.

But before I even got close, I felt a huge wrench in my stomach, and Ares glowed gold, his movements speeding up so much I could barely see him. Fatigue and dizziness washed over me and I staggered, my charge broken like I'd hit a wall.

The golden blur in front of me wobbled, my eyelids suddenly heavy, and it took everything I had not to fall to my knees.

"Fucking... asshole..." I tried to say, but the words came out as a whisper.

I felt as though I'd been hit by a truck, and to my dismay, I couldn't stop my knees from buckling. The blur of gold that was Ares faded from my vision as the red mist leaked away, everything replaced by a pale haze.

He was draining me. I didn't know how I knew that, but I was sure it was happening, because the only solid thing my fast receding senses could still feel was the fierce pull in the pit of my stomach.

He was using all of my power. Everything I had. To defeat the enemies I had disarmed, with the weapon I had enabled him to get.

A tinge of red crept back into the edges of my vision, the white haze clearing ever so slightly.

A gong sounded, so loud I half-lifted my hands to my ears, but found they were too heavy to get that far, so I let them fall again, my whole torso swaying. The roar of a crowd penetrated my ears, and the pull in my stomach lessened so abruptly that I lost my balance somehow, pitching forward onto my elbows.

I took a shuddering breath, trying to see clearly, but everything was too blurry, and my eyelids simply wouldn't do what I needed them to do. A shadow moved over me, and my instincts kicked in. Blind and half immobile or not, today was not the day a one-eyed fuckwit killed me. I dropped onto my side, my limbs feeling like they weighed a ton as I dragged them into myself, and kicked up pathetically at the figure looming over me. My steel toe caps rang against metal, and I heard Ares.

"Stand up."

I tried to roll again, but I simply didn't have the strength. That kick had finished me. Frustration and anger hit me so hard that the back of my useless eyes burned hot with tears. I was fucking laid on the ground in front of the world I wanted to belong to, weak as a damned kitten.

"I hate you," I whispered. "You fucking did this to me." Then for the second time in two days, I passed out.

21

BELLA

"You really are a fucking moron, Ares. Learn to control yourself." The voice was vaguely familiar as it pushed its way through my consciousness.

"That's rich coming from you! I didn't know she was still so weak," I heard Ares snap back.

"I'm not weak," I said, but it came out a thick mumble. I pushed myself up onto my elbows and looked around. I was lying on another damned stone table, but this time the room was gloomy and bare, the surrounding walls all the same color as the stone the gladiator pit was made from.

Eris stepped into my line of vision, holding out a simple stone cup.

"My brother is a fool," Eris muttered.

"Why are you helping me?" I croaked, gulping at the liquid. It was nectar, and knowing how much better it would make my exhausted body feel, I glugged it greedily. I felt like death warmed up, every muscle aching like hell.

"As much as I like to watch him flail around like a child, I don't actually want to see him killed. And without you, he has fuck all."

"You know he's using my power then?" I glanced sideways at Ares. Fierce fury leapt inside me but my exhausted body couldn't fight and rage like it usually did, and a wave of pain beat through my head as I gripped the stone cup hard enough to make my fingers ache.

I looked away from him, back to Eris.

"Yes," she said. "Everyone out there does now, too. It was pretty obvious when you went down like a sack of shit."

I heard a hiss from the God of War, and forced myself to drink more nectar instead of looking at him. Zeeva jumped up beside me as I swallowed the smooth liquid. It wasn't working yet.

"Why are you here? You always show up too damn late," I said to the cat.

"I have changed my position on helping you." I paused, raising my eyebrows at Zeeva. Even that small movement made my head hurt more. *"Do not respond out loud. We will talk more later."*

I did as she said, finishing what was left in the cup and feeling a tiny surge in strength. Enough for my simmering rage to take hold.

"So just to recap, Ares drained all of my energy and power to defeat three cyclopes that I had already disarmed alone," I said loudly.

"Yes. And now neither of you will have any power at all in the next fight," said Eris, in a patronizing tone I knew was meant for her brother.

"I-" started Ares, but trailed off.

"How long until the next fight?" I asked.

"Half an hour."

"I want a moment alone with Ares."

The words surprised me even as I said them. I didn't even want to lay eyes on him, never mind be alone with him. But the fury whirling through me needed an outlet before my head exploded, and if I couldn't physically expend it, I would have to do something else.

"I'll bet you do," Eris said, then wheeled away from me and strode through a rough stone doorway. I watched her curvy leather-clad ass swing out of the room and took a deep breath, trying to channel some of her sass through my fatigued system. Zeeva jumped down off the stone table, gave me a lingering look, then sauntered off after Eris.

"If you are expecting an apology-" began Ares, but as my eyes snapped to his, he stopped speaking. He wasn't wearing his helmet so his reaction on seeing my face was clear.

"You are surprised by how angry I am?" I hissed. "You, who shares my power, who knows what it is like to fight and win, to revel in strength and victory, are surprised to see me so angry when you drained me of all my strength and let me crumple helpless to the ground in front of the fucking world?"

More blood pounded in my head, the rage making it throb harder. Ares' mouth set in a hard line, and he dropped his gaze from mine.

"I have not been able to use my power in a fight for some time," he said quietly, still not meeting my eyes.

"You're a fucking god, not a child! How can you have so little control of yourself? And at someone else's expense?" I spat. I mean, I'd lost control before, of course I had, but I hadn't hurt someone who didn't deserve it since I was a teenager.

I saw anger in Ares' eyes as they flicked to mine, but it died out fast as I glared at him. "What is done is done. We must now work out how to survive," he said flatly.

"Fuck you, Ares. I can't fight with you. I can't work with you. If you had helped me smash the staffs in the first place you'd have got the sword faster, and we both could have taken out the cyclopes, but you insisted on acting like an arrogant asshole."

"We have to work together," he ground out.

"Why? I'm no damned use to you like this!" I yelled, gesturing at my aching body, anger reaching fever pitch. Feeling so useless was burning a hole in my gut, in my *soul*. I always had my fighting spirit, my speed and strength. Not having it was unbearable. "You've taken everything out of me, right before a fight! Do you know how that feels?"

"Yes!" He shouted back at me so loudly that my churning fury was momentarily halted. "I know exactly how that feels," he roared. "I have been living with it for months! Zeus stole my power and to taste it again from you is-" He stamped his foot, snapping his mouth closed as if he'd said too much. He rubbed a hand across his face, his long hair falling over his shoulder, and an unexpected stab of empathy jolted through me.

He'd gotten carried away in the fight. He got a taste of the thing he missed most in the world, and he got carried away. I could understand that, on some level.

But not at another's expense.

"I won't fight with you. I won't help you. I can't. You were right before. We'll get each other killed."

Joshua's face filled my mind as I spoke, pouring guilt over my boiling anger, but I knew my words were true. We *would* get each other killed if we carried on like this, and then I'd be unable to help anyone. Ares was rash and selfish and impossible. I would just have to rely on his huge ego to be justified and pray he could defeat the Lord's tests without power. There was no doubt he was a good fighter and could withstand pain, magic or none.

I felt sick as I thought about watching him from the sidelines, Joshua's life at stake and me doing nothing, but I couldn't see another way if he was going to treat me like this.

"I do not believe I can win this fight without your help," Ares said after a long pause, almost too quietly for me to hear.

"I have no power left for you to use! And that's *your* damned fault!"

"That is why I need you. With no power, I need your help. To fight whatever we are to face next."

I blinked at him. Had I heard that right? He was

looking down at his feet, his huge arms folded across his chest.

"You need my help to fight? Not to just use me as a fucking battery whenever you feel like it, but to actually fight?"

He looked up at me, and the look in his eyes made my eyebrows rise even higher. He looked... normal. Like a normal guy, asking for something he hoped he would get.

"I do not know what a battery is," he said.

The simplicity of his statement took me by surprise. "A battery is a power source in my world," I said quietly.

"Oh. Then yes. I would like you to help me fight whatever Pain is going to put in the pit with me next, not as a battery."

I stared at him. I wasn't getting an apology, that much was clear. But I reckoned this was as good as the same thing from a god. He was asking, politely, for my help and he wouldn't do that unless he wanted me to get killed, or actually thought I could fight.

I narrowed my eyes at him. "Are you trying to get me killed so that you get my power that way?"

He pulled an affronted face. "If I was going to kill you, I would do it with honor."

"Like over the dead body of my friend?"

"That is not how I had planned to kill you," he answered gruffly. I held my hand up, signaling him to stop.

"Look, if you actually want my help, telling me how you had planned to kill me is a bad idea."

"Agreed."

"Would you look at that. We actually agree on something," I muttered. The sincere look in his eyes, the absence of angry defensiveness, along with my intense desire to *not* walk away from all of this had mounted up, and somehow my anger was melting away. It was almost as though him turning his anger off had also turned off mine.

Truth of the matter was, I wanted to fight. I had a point to prove to that crowd now. If Ares really was willing to work with me, instead of getting us both killed, we could likely give them a show to remember.

"After this test, we need to talk properly about my power. And you are never, ever to drain me like that again."

I saw him bristle at being spoken to so authoritatively, the muscles in his jaw working. "It was an accident," he said eventually.

"Is that you swearing not to do it again? 'Cos it didn't sound like it."

His eyes locked on mine and a new intensity burned in his irises. I couldn't tell if it was anger or regret or something else completely, but whatever it was he was feeling it hard. I resisted the urge to look away.

"I swear," he said, through gritted teeth.

"Fine. I... I'm very tired," I said, tearing my eyes from his uncomfortable gaze and swinging my legs awkwardly over the table. I tested my weight on them. My thighs felt like I had run three marathons and my feet throbbed, but I could stand. "I don't actually know how much help I can be."

"Have more nectar. It should take effect before the next fight, though it will probably not have time to restore your magic." He moved toward me, leaning close to pick up my empty stone cup. It was impossible not to notice that he smelled of fresh sweat and sand and metal. I closed my eyes a second, getting a grip on myself, then pivoted to watch him move to another table in the long room, where a jug stood.

He poured me a drink and passed it over, and I drank, relieved to have something to concentrate on. My stomach was tying itself in knots. Residual adrenaline, anticipation for the next fight and lingering shame at my public display of weakness all crowded for space in my head. But the thing that was taking up the most space in my fuzzy brain, the thing stamping around and sending my rational thoughts scattering?

Bone-deep confusion over the mountain of muscle kicking at the sand before me.

What he had just done was selfish, dangerous, and made me so angry that I thought I was going to explode. But I was connected to him somehow, in a way that made everything else lose its sense.

"What is this place?" Bella asked me, as she sipped more nectar.

"It is where the fighters used to eat when they lived under the pits," I told her. The remnants of her power were still coursing through me, and just keeping my voice level wasn't easy. To feel the blissful elation of speed and strength and movement when I'd been fighting the cyclopes and drawing on her magic... I had told her the truth. I had never meant to drain her of all her power and energy.

But now I was worried that my lack of power was doing something else to me. This girl meant nothing to me, yet an alien feeling was gripping my entire chest every time I looked at her now.

Guilt.

I felt guilty about what I had done to her.

Before Zeus stole my power, I would not have given a second thought to it. I didn't kill her, I just left her weak, so that I may demonstrate my power. Bask in glory. That was what I did best. So why did I feel like I had done something wrong?

Because I knew the shame she would have felt, collapsing weak to the ground. I knew the thrill of the fight that I had denied her. I understood it in a way that only she and I could.

I shook off the thought, disliking what it might mean. My lack of power must have been affecting my head, as well as my body. It was making me weak everywhere. I could not afford to worry about others, when I had such a difficult goal to achieve.

But that was exactly why I did have to worry about her. As much as I hated it, I couldn't do this alone.

I just wished it wasn't her. I wished that the fire in her eyes didn't linger there in my memories for hours after each fight I had with her. I wished that I didn't hear the drums of war every time she lost her temper. I wished that her fierce tenacity didn't spark respect inside me.

No, my feelings were wrong. So wrong. She was a human. An annoying, tiny human. I compared her to Aphrodite in my mind, picturing the two side-by-side. The Goddess of Love and most beautiful woman in the world was not even comparable to Bella. Clearly what I was feeling was a product of my situation. When I had my power back, my mind would strengthen again, and Aphrodite would love me again.

"Why don't the fighters live under here anymore?"

"They chose to live in their own camps." For once, I was grateful for her questions distracting me.

"Huh. I can understand that," Bella nodded. "If I

was a slave, I wouldn't want to live under rock. You'd feel more trapped wouldn't you?"

"I don't know," I answered.

"What do you mean you don't know? Think about it, if you were told you had no freedom at all, and you had to do everything someone else told you to, including fight for your life, you'd already be pretty miserable, right?"

"I- I don't know. I have never considered it." She gaped at me.

"Your realm allows slavery and you've 'never considered it'?"

"Well... No."

"Then consider it right now! Consider a life where you are somebody's damned toy! How can you never have put yourself in their shoes?"

"I don't need to. I'm a God."

"You're a ruler. These people are your responsibility."

"That is not how my world works. I let every King or Queen rule as they wish. It is not easy to earn a kingdom and it is even harder to hold on to one. They deserve to rule as they like." I folded my arms, satisfied with my answer.

"Survival of the fittest," she said thoughtfully. "I think it's wrong."

Anger surged through me. "You have been here two days! How can you possibly think you know more than me about my own world?"

"I don't, but it appears you're incapable of empathy. So you're not fit to rule."

Red tinged my vision. "You dare to tell me I am unfit to rule?"

"Until you consider what it is like to live the life your subjects do, yes. If you can imagine what they go through every day and still decide to rule that way, then that's different. I mean, you'd be an asshole, but a better ruler."

"Stop calling me that." Every time she used that word a frisson of energy moved all the way down my spine. I thought it was anger, but somehow the fact that she felt strongly enough about me to use such a word was oddly satisfying.

I didn't like it at all.

She shrugged and finished her drink. "I'm just saying, in a world like this you wouldn't have a problem filling the fighting pits with people who actually wanted to be there. Slavery is not necessary. You'd see that if you could understand what it would be like to be someone's slave."

Her words buzzed loudly in my mind. Sometimes, on my dark days, I did feel like someone else owned me. And I hated it. I instantly dismissed the thought though. Aphrodite loved me, she did not treat me as a slave. I made her happy when we made love. That was not the relationship of slave and master. I shook my head.

"You are infuriating," I said.

"I'm feeling better," she answered.

"Knock knock," called my sister's voice from the open doorway, before she strode in. "Not interrupting, are we?"

"How do you make your hair stay up on top of your head like that?" asked Bella, cocking her head at Eris' mountain of curls.

"How is that important?" I asked her incredulously. The girl was insane. "Will you ever stop asking questions?"

Eris laughed. "I'll show you one day. If you survive this." I heard the undercurrent of nerves in her voice. And she was right to have them. Bella didn't seem to be aware of how unlikely it was that we could defeat a magical creature without any power at all. More guilt and shame trickled through me. It was my fault. Getting so caught up in that blissful feeling of her magic might cost us our lives. And now I had asked her to join me in a fight I wasn't sure we could win. If she died, it would be my fault completely.

But I'd seen her fight and the truth was, I had a better chance of winning with her than without her.

When I'd had my power I would not have mourned the loss of one human in a bid to strengthen myself. I had to be strong, like I used to be. I had to win back Aphrodite's respect.

And besides, if Bella found out how she became human, I would have to kill her anyway, before she killed me.

23

BELLA

The doubt in Eris' eyes was seriously unsettling.

"Surely we can defeat whatever Pain throws at us?" I said, my usual bluster and confidence returning now that I'd finished my second cup of nectar. Thank god.

"It will be a creature or being with power, designed to face a god. Fighting with no power at all will be... difficult," said Ares. To hear doubt in his voice was far, far more worrying.

"Then we'll have to be smart as well as tough," I said. "If you'd listened to me last time-"

He cut me off. "Then I would have got the sword easier, I know!"

"Christ on a cracker, calm down armor-boy," I said, giving him a look.

"I must say, it's more fun to see you get pissed with your helmet off," said Eris with a smile. "Your jaw does this excellent twitching thing."

"You've seen my face many times before," he grunted.

"Yeah, but not with someone else around who riles you as much as she does. It's fun." She grinned and hopped up onto the stone table swinging her legs. Her enormous boobs were squished into a leather wrap-around thing that she must have been sewn into, it was so tight.

"Look, my point is that I don't think Pain's tests will just be about brute strength. He embodies pain, they will be endurance tests, that will hurt. In the last test, it was about taking the pain of smashing the staffs to get ahead. We can handle that without magic, right?"

"I can handle any pain," said Ares, standing straighter.

"You're about to find out what it feels like to be human, little brother," drawled Eris.

By the time I was following Ares through a maze of rock tunnels, heading for the sandy stage and whatever foe awaited us, I was feeling much better. I didn't know if I would get any of my usual focus, or accelerated speed or strength, but the sheer volume of adrenaline buzzing through me would hopefully make up for that.

Knowing that Eris and Ares, ancient all-powerful deities, were worried about our ability to win this fight was only spurring me on. I had a point to prove to both the crowd and the godly siblings.

The thing about years of fighting people much, much bigger than myself was that I'd had to develop a confidence in the skills I had that they didn't. If it weren't for my inexorable need for confrontation, I would never have stepped into the ring with most of my opponents. On paper, I should have lost every single fight. And that's why people came to see me. It took four or five fights in every shady shithouse I found to compete in before the bookies realized what they had on their hands.

I'd smash my first opponent to bits and they would think it was a fluke, a lucky break. They'd pitch me against somebody harder, and when I made short work of them, the odds against me would decrease just a little, but I would still be far from the favorite to win. After seeing me knock out another three guys twice my size, pumped up to the eyeballs on steroids, the odds would finally tip, and I would become the favorite. At which point I always left, to find a new challenge, a new group of lowlifes and adrenaline junkies to shock and delight.

The reason I always won wasn't because I was stronger or faster, although I often was. It was because I had learned what made me different. I didn't start out winning. I had my ass handed to me plenty of times at the beginning. But slowly I realized that fighting wasn't just about having big muscles. Pain wasn't just about taking blows.

Strength of mind was what had always given me the edge; unbending confidence, and an ability to see from another's point of view. And that would be what gave me the edge in this fight too. I had to be the reason Ares won this.

I had to be. Because if I could make him see how good I was, he would have to help me with my power. He would have to concede that I was more useful with it than without it.

I repeated that in my head as I walked, trying to make it louder than the traitorous part of me that wanted him to see how good I was simply because I was desperate to impress him.

The roar of the crowd as we stepped out of one of the gates onto the sandy stage was deafening. They were cheering for Ares of course, the golden blur who had devastated the three cyclops half an hour earlier.

I stood straighter as he waved the sword he had won at the crowd. The red plume on his helmet fluttered as he moved, and I couldn't help rolling my eyes. I was developing an unnatural resentment of his helmet, and I had no idea why.

It's because it covers his beautiful face, the sex-starved part of my brain piped up. I ground my teeth together. Maybe the extraordinarily high levels of excitement and adrenaline I had experienced since coming to Olympus had done something to my sex drive.

Or maybe I had just met the first man in the world who could handle me.

"Are you ready, mighty God of War?" boomed Pain's voice, and I pulled my knife from my pocket, focusing. It was time to prove to everyone what I was made of.

"Hephaestus has provided me with a monster fit for a God for your second round!" Pain's voice was filled with glee.

"Hephaestus makes creatures from metal," Ares said to me, moving so that his back was to mine.

"More electricity then?" I asked.

"I doubt he would use the same trick twice," he growled back. The ground rumbled for the second time, but when I looked to the gates, they remained closed. "Move!" barked Ares, and I realized with a jolt that the center of the pit was dropping. We both moved fast, reaching the edge of the ring where the ground was stable and turning back. The middle section of the pit had dropped too far to be able to see what was down there, and I began to step cautiously toward the edge, to peer down. Ares' arm shot out across my front, stopping me.

"But-" I started and he shook his head, plume bouncing.

"It will rise again in a moment. Carrying our foe."

"Oh." This must be common in the pits then. "Should we spread out?"

"No. If it is entering the pit this way, then it is too large for the gates. We should stay where we can communicate."

My surprise at his willingness to work together was only dampened slightly by my alarm that we would be fighting something too big to fit through the gates. They were eight feet tall at least. What the fuck was coming?

. . .

I didn't have to wait long to find out. I saw its head first, rising from the hole in the middle of the pit. Made from shining metal, the back of its serpentine head was ringed with vicious-looking horns, and black oily liquid dripped from silver fangs. Adding to its snakelike appearance, the head was attached to a long neck, and I held my breath to see if it would be followed by a body with limbs, or if it actually was a snake.

It wasn't a snake. It was much, much worse than a snake.

The neck *was* attached to a body. A huge hulking body with four legs ending in lethally clawed feet. But that wasn't what was causing my pulse to rocket and my heart to pound in my chest. There were two other heads attached to the body. Three long necks wound around each other as the heads snapped and snarled at us and very real fear trickled down my spine, my breath quickening.

"Say hello to my new Hydra!" sang Pain.

"Don't cut off any heads!" Ares said urgently. I gaped at him.

"What the fuck do you think I'll be cutting them off with?" I held up my tiny flick-blade as the Hydra made an awful screeching sound. Ares' eyes darted to the little weapon, then back to me.

"For every one head removed, two grow back," he said.

"You're the one with the sword," I snapped. "How the hell are we going to kill it?"

"I've only seen one before, and it was disabled by someone pulling out the power source in its head."

The pit floor was almost level again, and I didn't think we'd have long once it was flat before the Hydra charged. "How do we get up to its head?" I was estimating its height at about twelve feet easily. My usual red mist, and calm focus wasn't coming. My breath was short, and my hyped up heart-rate was making my limbs shake.

I dragged at the blind confidence I had felt just moments ago, trying to fill myself with it. I had to prove myself. *I had to prove myself.*

"I don't know. And we have to work out which head."

"Shit."

"Are you ready?" Ares asked, dropping his stance and leveling his sword at the Hydra.

Nope, but I sure as fuck wasn't going to admit that to him. "Course," I said, mimicking him, trying not to think about how under-armed I was. I loved my knife, I really did, but it had never, ever felt so inadequate. I was up against a twelve foot tall monster made of metal. It would *so* not be my first choice of weapon.

The thought actually hardened my resolve though, as the Hydra screeched again, and the pit of the floor finally clicked into place. Shoving my knife back into my pocket, I flexed my hands into fists, and the creature stamped and shuffled on the sand. This would have to be about speed and agility.

Your body is a weapon, your body is a weapon, I chanted. It was what I had told myself in prison, the only time I had been separated from my blade.

All three Hydra heads stopped squirming and

locked on us. My skin tingled and my limbs shook with adrenaline, blood crashing in my ears. Before it could charge us though, Ares bellowed a roar, and launched himself forward. Abandoning all doubt to the dust, I screamed and followed him.

I saw instantly what he planned to do. As the metal beast powered forward to meet us, Ares dropped, skidding across the sand and raising his sword high above him in a point. He was going for the underbelly. Seizing the opportunity he was giving me by distracting it, I veered to the right. If I could get behind it, I would have a shot at climbing up its back. That had to be the easiest way of getting to one of the heads.

But I underestimated the creature. The head closest to me darted out as I reached it, and I heard Ares' sword make contact with the metal. A shriek accompanied the shredding sound, but I couldn't see if the cry had come from Ares or the Hydra because a freaking horned snake head twice the size of my own was snapping at me, metal fangs as long as my forearms glistening with black ooze. I tried to turn on a burst of speed but none came, and the thing caught the back of my ribs as I raced on. The impact was enough that I went flying forward, mercifully out of the thing's reach, but painfully hard enough to totally screw up my landing. Pain lanced up through my ankle as I stumbled and fell, twisting it. I felt my face screw up as I rolled, turning so that I could see if the Hydra was still after me.

It wasn't. All three heads were now trying to get under its own body as Ares crouched beneath it, slashing and stabbing with his sword.

"Get on its back!" he hollered.

I threw a glare at him as I scrabbled to my feet. Thank fuck for the toughened leather armor. If it was a fang that had caught my back, it would have gone straight through flesh. I tested my weight on my ankle, and though darts of pain sprang up my shin, it wasn't debilitating. I first jogged, then ran toward the Hydra, taking care to stay behind it, out of reach of its long necks. But as I got close it began to stamp its feet hard, and a wave of heat washed over me.

I kept running as one head shot up high, reaching over the creature's back and locking eyes on me. It opened its jaws wide, and an unearthly glow shone from deep in its throat. Uneasiness gripped me, and I tore my eyes from the head to its tail. I needed to climb up its tail to its back, and I could worry about why its mouth was glowing later.

I was only a few feet away. Spikes jutted up along the Hydra's whole spine, and the metal it was made of what looked to be millions of tiny interlocking scales. I threw myself at its haunches as I reached it and cried out at the fierce heat of the material under my touch. But I held on, jamming my fingertips into the tiny gaps between the scales, and kicking with my feet to try to push myself higher.

I could hear Ares yelling but I couldn't make out the words over the shrill screeching noise the Hydra was making. With an effort, I managed to pull myself up onto the thing's back, just in time to see all three heads twist over to look at me. The wailing noise wasn't coming from any of them, I realized. It was coming from three small glowing metal stumps at the creature's shoulders. I watched with horror as the metal scales duplicated themselves out of nowhere, the stumps rapidly turning into necks.

I had about thirty seconds until heads formed on the end of them, I realized. And then there would be six freaking sets of fangs to deal with. I lurched forward, trying to reach for the central neck whilst staying low enough to avoid the snapping jaws, but the heads on the left and right had different ideas. They swooped in on either side of me, and I conceded with a second to spare that I couldn't avoid them. I gritted my teeth and threw myself off the Hydra's back, hearing a satisfying crunching sound as the left and right head smashed into each other, before my shoulder smacked into the ground, swiftly followed by the rest of me.

"Where did the new heads come from?" I heard Ares yell, then felt a tug on my arm that stopped me rolling through the dust. Within seconds he had yanked me to my feet, and we were running to the edge of the pit.

"I don't know," I panted, looking at him. Dark oily stuff covered his gleaming armor. "But I can't get to one head while the others aren't distracted. They're too quick."

"We'll have to try something else." We both looked at the Hydra. If it wasn't trying to kill me, I'd have thought the last metal fangs clicking into place as the new heads finished building themselves was cool as hell. As it *was* trying to kill me, I was stuck somewhere between crazy impressed and freaking terrified.

"How the hell are we going to get past six heads?" I breathed. As if hearing me, the creature pawed at the ground, its claws scraping on the stone, then took a slow step toward us. All six fanged jaws snapped in unison, then opened wide. They were glowing again. The sound around us changed, and I realized it was because the steady roar of cheers and whoops from the crowd had hushed.

The Hydra was getting ready for the kill.

24

ARES

The feeling burning through my body as I watched the Hydra heads rear back up before us was not fear. I knew that for certain. But it was nothing I had ever experienced before.

It was connected to fear, perhaps. A kind of fear-fueled excitement? It made my heart hammer against my ribcage, my stomach clench in anticipation, my breathing quicken. I could feel sweat on the back of my neck, cool on my skin. I could hear blood rushing in my ears.

Eris' words rang through my head. "You are about to find out what it feels like to be human." Was that was this was? This visceral, physical reaction to the threat before us? It was... intense. Never, ever before had I not known I could beat my opponent. Never before had I been so out of control of my own fate. And contrary to everything I thought I would feel, *it was delicious.*

I could die. Actually die. The towering creature

before me could end my life if I wasn't smart enough, strong enough, fast enough. The thought set my heart racing even harder, as though it were trying to remind me that keeping it beating was my challenge.

I felt a twisted grin take my face, resolution coursing through my body, hardening my muscles. This was a real fight. A real, true, life-or-death fight. Could there be anything more thrilling than overcoming death itself? How had I never known this desire for glory, this need to believe in my own ability? If I could beat the Hydra, the six-headed, twelve-foot-tall monster that by all rights should crush me to dust, I would be an actual hero. A deserved hero.

Fiery excitement caused a noise to bubble from my lips, and Bella snapped her head to look at me. Was she feeling this too? Did she feel this every time she fought?

The idea was intoxicating.

A wave of heat rippled through the pit, grounding me ever so slightly. Something was about to happen. In a sudden blur of movement all six heads shot forward, black liquid firing from the lethal jaws. The oily substance coated the ground, not quite reaching us but spreading fast.

"I'm gonna guess that we don't want to touch that stuff," said Bella. I glanced at the exposed parts of her arms, then down at my own solid armor. Even without my magic, my armor would withstand more than her human-made boots and leather. If the liquid was acid or lava, she was in trouble.

"Climb onto my shoulders. From up there you may

be able to reach the heads, and you will not make contact with the liquid.

She stared at me. "Climb on your shoulders? Seriously?"

"Yes. Do it now."

"But-" she started, then yelled and looked down, leaping sideways. The liquid had reached her boot, and as I had feared, instantly began burning through the material, acrid smoke sizzling from her shoe. I looked down at my own divinely created boots, relieved to see they were not reacting to the acid. "Get it off me!" Bella kicked and shook her leg, bending to untie the shoe fast, until a shriek from the Hydra made us both look up. It was charging.

With a fierce curse, Bella gave me a glare, then reached for my shoulder. I bent as she lifted the boot that wasn't covered in the black liquid, cupped one hand beneath it and lifted. I heard her intake of breath as she clambered across my shoulders, then felt my own breath constrict as her thighs moved around my neck. But I had no time to deal with the new increase in pulse rate her thighs were causing. The Hydra had reached us.

I slashed with my sword, no longer caring if I severed a neck, as I raced to my left. Bella shouted, one of her hands gripping my helmet as I ran. The black acid splashed up around me as my gold boots pounded the earth, the Hydra stamping and shrieking behind me.

"We need to get under it!" shouted Bella. Her voice sounded strained.

"We need to go for the heads!" I roared back. I saw one of her boots, only half of it remaining and smoking, fly to the ground in my peripheral vision.

"No, this is a test of pain, and the burning acid is on the ground. We have to endure the acid to win, the answer is low, not high!"

I processed her words as I darted out of the way of a snapping jaw, trying to ignore the feel of her legs squeezing around my neck. She was right before, about the staffs, though I wouldn't admit it. It made sense, I decided. I would do as she bid me.

"You can't touch the ground, you'll burn. Let me slide under, and you can stand on my armor."

"You're sure you can take the acid?" She gripped my helmet harder as I pivoted one-eighty and held my sword high. I felt her move on my shoulders, her feet coming up to where her thighs were.

"My armor is divine. It can withstand anything!" I roared, and ran full-pelt at the creature.

Excitement set my insides alight as the myriad horned snake heads snapped down toward us and I dropped, putting my trust in Bella to both stay off the acid and avoid the fangs. She jumped as I slid from my rear-end to my back, flying under the belly of the beast as scaled necks collided with each other, acid splashing up in waves either side of me.

Bella gave a true battle cry, raising her arms above her and grabbing onto the scaled underbelly of the creature. I jammed my sword into the ground to stop my movement, trying to maneuver myself underneath her as she hung from her fingertips, keeping her legs bent and feet from touching the acid below. Finding one of the gashes I had made earlier with my sword, she pushed one arm deep into the creature, holding on with a strength I hadn't thought her small frame capable of.

Her body convulsed suddenly, in time with a shriek from the Hydra, and the four clawed feet around me began to stamp and jump in earnest. A scream, high and long ripped through my skull, and when I realized it was coming from her I shouted her name before I could stop myself.

"Bella!" She didn't respond, her body convulsing again, but her arm moving further into the mechanical creature, then wrenching back hard. She dropped, slamming into my armored chest in an awkward crouch, and the brief glimpse I got of her agonized face, tears streaming down her cheeks, set a boiling swell of rage through me, before she began to slide on the gleaming metal.

I dropped the sword, flinging both arms out to stop her falling, pulling her body flat to mine. "Hold on to me!" She cried out in pain, and for a moment I thought she had touched the acid. Then she pulled her left arm free of my vice-like grip, the one that had been inside the Hydra. The skin was searing red and blistered, but clutched in her fist was a pulsing purple orb.

"It's dead," she gasped, and with a flash of light the metal beast above us vanished, a gong sounding loud in my ears.

25

BELLA

Ares sat up, gripping me around the waist with one arm and gently moving my legs with his other so that he could scoop them up, clear of the black acid. Tears of pain still leaked from my eyes, but I didn't care. The agony of my burned arm was blocking out everything other than the fact that I'd killed the Hydra.

"How did you do it?" Ares asked me quietly as he stood, still cradling me.

I screwed my face up against the fierce burning, and concentrated on answering him. "Followed the heat. Put my arm in, went to where it was hottest." A wave of nausea took me and I clamped my mouth shut. Agony or none, I didn't want to throw up on the God of War's fancy armor.

"Pain! We have defeated your test!" Ares bellowed. The crowd erupted in response to his words. "That is enough for today."

"Indeed. Good show," came Pain's magnified voice, then everything flashed white.

We were in the caravanserai, in my room, and Ares set me down on the bed quickly. More nausea crawled up my throat.

"I feel sick," I croaked, and he dropped to his knees beside the bed, before popping back up with my rucksack clutched in his huge fist. He rummaged through it fast, his armor clanking, then pulled a tub of the paste that we had got at the apothecary out of it.

"This may hurt," he said, putting the tub next to me on the bed, then pulling his helmet off. The pain was so all-consuming that I couldn't even focus on his face. I felt like my arm-bones themselves were burning, my entire forearm and hand a mass of fire and agony. I was getting flashes of brief and blessed numbness, but I knew on some level that that was not good. "Are you ready?" Ares asked me. I nodded.

He was right. It did hurt. In fact, it hurt more than anything else I'd ever experienced in my life. More than when I'd broken my ribs, my collarbone, my ankle. I was sick. I cried. I screamed. I was a damned mess.

But Ares sat beside me patiently, applying more thick paste to my raw and scalded skin, and saying nothing but the words, "You can sleep soon."

After what felt like an eternity my arm was

completely covered in the stuff, and thank all the gods, I stopped feeling like I was being flayed alive and started to feel the cooling effect of the paste. Within a minute of the pain lessening, I was unconscious, the sleep Ares had been promising taking me completely.

When I woke, the first thing I registered was pain. But it wasn't agonizing, just dull and uncomfortable. With an instinctive delicacy, I lifted my arm clear of my body, and sat up slowly. Although very similar, this room was not my own. The closet and washroom door were the wrong way around. I looked around slowly, stopping as my gaze fell on Ares. He was sitting in a large and extravagantly upholstered chair, wearing an open linen shirt and leaning one elbow on the armrest. He looked... disheveled.

"How is your arm?" he asked me. I blinked at him, then looked to my raised limb. The paste had hardened, forming some sort of cast. I was grateful for that. I didn't want to see the state of my skin underneath.

"It hurts," I said. "But not as bad as before."

I felt a tiny tug in my gut and I snapped my eyes to him. "What are you doing?"

"Helping you," he said gruffly. "Zeeva said I had to let you sleep for your power to restore properly." Anger started to bubble inside me.

"You've just been helping me so that you can get to my magic?"

He gave a hiss of annoyance and stood up, coming to the bed. *His* bed, I realized with a start. If we weren't in my room, we must be in his. "No. You needed your power back for me to do this." He leaned over me and took my other hand. My body reacted to his touch immediately, my pulse quickening of its own volition. I felt a stronger pull in my stomach, but before I could open my mouth to protest or question him, delicious soothing pulses washed through my arm. A tingle that wasn't tickly or exciting, but completely relaxing, moved all the way from my spine and down my arm, and every muscle in my body went slack as I melted into the mattress.

For the first time since we had entered the gladiator pit, nothing in my body hurt.

"Gods have healing powers," Ares said quietly, then let go of my hand. He didn't move away though, his hair falling forward as he leaned over me.

"Even Gods of War?" I whispered, the soothing warmth fading, but no pain returning.

"Especially Gods of War. I had to wait until you regained your magic to use it though."

"Why didn't you do that with the manticore sting?"

"You were unconscious. I can't use your power whilst you're unconscious. And besides, healing a burn is not the same as healing poison. You're still not that strong."

I tried to get indignant about being told I wasn't strong, but failed. He wasn't insulting me. He was stating fact.

He had helped me. Nursed me. Why? For my power, obviously. But who'd have thought he would be so gentle? I looked into his eyes, wondering how anyone could look so sad and fierce at the same time. But then, I had been both sad and fierce most of my life. "Thank you," I said.

He straightened, moving away from me a little. "You were injured with honor. You killed the Hydra."

"You're damn right I did," I grinned at him. "Who needs magic, eh?"

"We do, to heal you," he said, and my elation drooped a little. "You need to wash off the paste, it is no longer necessary."

I frowned at my arm. "Shouldn't I leave it there to protect the skin a bit longer?"

"Your skin is healed."

"What?"

"The healing doesn't just take away the pain, it heals your wounds. Your arm is fine now."

I stared at Ares, the impact of his words crashing into me. "You can instantly heal wounds here?"

"Not everyone can. My sister can't, for example. Her power is too destructive."

"But... What's the point in fighting if you can just heal?"

Ares faltered, his gaze dropping from mine. When his eyes found mine again, embers were dancing in his irises, but I felt no anger from him. "I am immortal. Today was the first time in millennia that I fought with the real risk of not just injury, but death." The excitement in his low voice was infectious, and I felt my stomach tense as I recalled the rush of adrenaline that accompanied the build up to a challenge. "It was glorious."

"So for thousands of years you've never been at risk of losing?" He licked his lips as he shook his head, and heat flashed in my core. "No wonder you're so fucking miserable," I said on a long breath. "It's one of the best feelings in the world. The knowledge that if you best your opponent, you've earned it. The challenge laid out before you, the odds stacked against you." All my muscles were tensing now, my pain gone completely, and my energy returned in force.

My chance to bask in the glory of my victory over the Hydra had been stolen by my injury, and now the elation was flooding me in a blissful tidal wave.

"I felt truly alive today," Ares said. "And watching you fight with such courage despite having no power at all..." He stared into my eyes and the beat of a drum banged in the depths of my mind.

I had done it. I had won the God of War's respect.

Only it wasn't his respect I wanted now. The energy pouring through my body was all going to one damned place, and I couldn't stop my eyes moving from his, down to his mouth, then further down, tracing the lines of his abs, the V of the muscles cording his stomach and hips, the low band of his pants.

The drums got louder, and when Ares took a ragged breath I knew for certain that he could hear them too. Before I could stop myself, I wrapped my good hand around the back of his head and pulled him to me, closing my lips over his. His hands came to my face immediately, his fingers pushing into my hair as his tongue found mine and pleasure exploded in my center, so fiercely I ached. My skin sprang to life with a sensitivity I'd never felt, every caress of his fingers on my neck and jaw sending shivers of pleasure through me.

He kissed me with the ferocity of a man starved, as though he had never tasted anything like me before, and I knew that because it was exactly how I felt. Never, *ever* had a kiss been so consuming, so full of promise, so damned *right*.

26

BELLA

I pulled him closer to me, his soft lips moving harder against mine, and he half-fell to the bed. His hand moved to my ribs as he rolled, the movement breaking the kiss, and fevered panic gripped me at the void he left. But his strong arms dragged me back to him, one hand now up my back, the other in my hair, pulling my head gently back so he could trail kisses down my throat.

I couldn't even comprehend how much I wanted him, shivers like electricity shooting from wherever his lips landed to all the places my body was screaming to be touched. As my nipples hardened I became vaguely aware that I was still wearing the supple corset. We were on our sides, my good arm now beneath him, and my left useless in its paste cast. I needed to feel his hard chest, his muscular back, his tanned skin. I longed to touch him, to feel all of him. The drums beat louder as my breath caught, his kisses reaching the bottom of my throat and moving toward my breasts. His hair brushed my skin tantalizingly as he moved.

He reached the top of the corset and stopped, looking up at my face, breathing as hard as I was. Flames, huge and fierce and hot and beautiful, were dancing in his eyes, and the sight was so fucking perfect that every single thing in my life that wasn't him faded into nothingness. Every thought, every doubt, every fact, even the freaking mattress beneath me ceased to exist - there was just him and me, our bodies belonging together, the need between my legs now painful in its intensity.

A deep moan left his lips, and he moved to kiss me, even hungrier than before.

"Ares? Persephone has come to heal Bella."

Eris' voice through the door startled us both, and Ares shot backwards so fast that he fell clean off the side of the huge bed. I scrabbled up to a sitting position, heat and arousal making my thoughts too slow to do anything useful. Ares got to his feet fast, and his eyes met mine. Though they were still filled with longing, the fire in his irises was dying out.

"We... We should not have done that."

The drums stopped.

I stared up at him, his words snapping my attention from the screaming need in my core.

"Why not?" I was breathing hard.

"Many reasons. We should not have done that." His words felt like a slap to the face. Did he need to say this whilst my lips were still swollen from kissing him?

My feelings must have shown on my face, because

his wild expression softened a second, before a hammering began on the door.

"Ares? Let us in," Eris called from the other side.

I pushed myself up from the mattress fast, feeling my cheeks beginning to burn. There was no way I wanted Eris or Persephone seeing me like this. And if this idiotic lump of muscle that called himself a man wanted to make me feel unwanted, he had succeeded.

"I'm showering," I mumbled, jumping off the bed and moving awkwardly fast to the washroom door. I slammed it shut behind me, hearing no protestation from Ares, then slumped against it, taking deep breaths and begging my body to settle down. After a moment's pause, I heard him speak.

"I used her own power to heal her, but thank you for coming, Queen Persephone."

I only just caught the Queen's response, something along the lines of being glad I was better and looking forward to seeing us at the ball in a few hours.

A ball? Fuck that. There was no way I was going to a damned party. I stamped across the beautiful bathroom to where an enormous sunken bath was set into the floor. I barely noticed the intricate orange and teal tiles lining the little pool as I yanked the faucets on.

How the fuck could I have been so stupid as to kiss him? More worryingly, how the fuck had it been so unbelievably good? If just a kiss was that sensational then what the hell would my body do if he got my clothes off?

He doesn't want to take my clothes off, I remembered,

the thought like a bucket of ice-cold water on my arousal. He just got carried away, again.

The man had no self-control at all. First he drained my power because it felt so good to have it again. Then he let the thrill of winning a fight he might actually have lost get the better of him. And me.

I kicked angrily at the water in the fast-filling pool, and snarled as my jeans got splashed. Tugging the tight denim off with one hand was hard enough, but getting the corset off was a freaking nightmare. By the time I was naked, I was ten times angrier than I had been before I started.

I sank into the pool, and my frustrations were momentarily halted when my arm met the water. The solid paste fizzed on my skin, and I flinched, expecting pain. But none came, and slowly the cast melted away. I gazed in wonder at my forearm, wiggling my fingers and lifting it from the bath.

It was perfect. As though I'd never hurt myself. An unstoppable excitement surged through me as I considered what being able to heal wounds like that would mean. Desire to get to my power swelled inside me, fighting for room with my anger.

In an effort to calm down, I tried to work out how I would feel if every fight I fought carried no risk at all. There was an array of powder blue and pink soaps on the side of the bath, and as I used them to wash the rest of the paste off my arm and then the sand and sweat from my body and my short blonde hair, I concentrated on what it would be like to be a goddess. Like really, properly thought about it, for the first time since this rollercoaster of chaos started.

Sure, being immortal would have its benefits. And being able to flash myself anywhere in the world would be cool as hell. So would the wealth and power that came with the position. Who didn't want to live in luxury?

But Ares had all of those things, and he was miserable. I didn't know exactly what it was that made him so humorless, but I knew it ran deeper than the loss of his power. His demeanor wasn't new, it was clearly deep set. He had no empathy at all. When we'd talked about the slaves earlier, he had obviously never even considered a life different than his own. Was that what power that mighty did to a person? Were all of the gods so deluded and out of touch?

And the kick he got from fighting the Hydra... He said he had not felt that feeling for millennia. Did I really want to give that up?

I let out a long sigh as I rinsed the suds from my hair. Ares was an ass. He had the body of a man, and the temperament of a teenager. Before I could think too long on just how manly his body was, I dragged my resolve firmly into place. If he thought us hooking up was a mistake, then so did I. Even if it *was* the hottest kiss known to man.

I was not interested in a guy who told a woman who was literally panting for him that he regretted kissing her.

No. Ares was a douche-bag. I would work with him

to finish the Trials and save Joshua, but no more ogling, drooling or fantasizing over him.

As far as my magic went... If I needed it to stay in Olympus, then so be it. But I was sure as hell not going to let it turn me into someone as messed up as him.

I pushed the washroom door open firmly, wearing my best 'fuck-off-I-don't-care-what-you-think' face. To my surprise, Ares was nowhere to be seen, but Eris was sitting on his bed instead.

"Thank the gods, I thought you were never going to leave that room," she drawled, standing up.

"Erm, why are you here?"

"Your hoity-toity cat asked me to help you get ready," she beamed. "I'm not usually up for helping people, but you fascinate me."

"Zeeva? Where is she?"

"Busy, apparently. Probably talking to someone else like they're complete shit, I suspect. Now, I've moved the clothes in your closet to this room."

"Wait, why?"

"Ares offered to swap rooms. Yours needed cleaning up after..." She trailed off, and I got an unpleasant flashback of heaving all over the floor as Ares treated my ruined flesh. A stab of something that wasn't anger for him knifed through my chest, and I screwed my face up.

"I don't need help getting ready. Where's my bag?"

"Sweetie, you definitely need help getting ready. Have you ever been to a ball in Olympus?"

"You know I haven't," I answered, my eyes flicking down to her ridiculous cleavage. She gave me a silky smile.

"I'm not going to put you in anything like this, I swear," she said. "You couldn't pull this look off anyway." I frowned and looked down at my boobs, wrapped in a large blue towel. They weren't as big as hers, granted, but they were OK. "No, I think we'll go for something feminine, yet badass," she mused.

Against all instructions from my brain, my mouth opened. "Like what?"

"There's plenty to choose from," she said, sauntering over to the closet and opening it. "Pick a color and I'll make it work." I cocked my head at her suspiciously.

"You're the Goddess of Discord and Chaos. I'm not sure I should be wearing anything you give me. It'll probably disintegrate half away through the evening and I'll be standing there naked."

"Now there's a thought!" Eris clapped her hands together. I rolled my eyes.

"Besides, I'm not going to any damned ball. I'm tired. And your brother is an asshole."

"You have to go, you're one of the guests of honor. And the aforementioned asshole is the other. So suck it up, and pick a color."

I was about to argue with her, but I already knew there was no point. Plus I wasn't really tired at all, and a part of me really wanted to find out what I might look like 'feminine, yet badass'. Ignoring the fact that it was the same part of me that wanted Ares to see me looking good, I stepped toward the closet.

"This one?" I pointed at a pale blue garment that had too many bits of fabric for me to work out what it was.

"Yes, that should work with your hair color," Eris mused, reaching out and picking up a lock of my wet hair. "But shoulder-length isn't right for you, sweetie."

"I'm not going any shorter," I said, stepping out of her reach, the hair slapping onto my cheek. It had taken me years to get it to grow this long, after I'd had to cut it super-short in prison. Long hair was too easy for others to use against you in a fight.

"No, no. Not shorter. Longer."

I felt a tingle across my scalp, then movement down my shoulders and back. I spun with a yelp, gripping my towel with one hand to stop it falling, and reaching around the back of my head with my other.

"What are you doing?" Eris grabbed my shoulder with one hand, stopping me turning in panicked circles and moved me in front of the long mirror that hung inside the open closet door.

I froze. My hair was long. Like waist-length long. And no longer one yellowish blob of color, but weaved with platinum and ash streaks, highlighted by the gentle waves it fell in. "Holy shit."

"Yeah. It's definitely an improvement. And I promise it won't all fall out."

"It's like supermodel hair," I breathed, too scared to touch it. "How did you do that?"

"Sweetie, I'm fucking ancient. There's not a lot I can't do."

"Ares said you can't heal," I said, remembering his words. A darkness crossed her face briefly.

"It's true my powers are mostly on the more destructive side." Her voice was slightly too hard as she spoke.

"Then how can you make beautiful hair? That's not destructive at all."

"Bella, making you look hot as hell will wreak plenty of havoc, trust me," she said, her sassy tone returning.

"What do you mean?" She stared at me, eyes full of mischief. I couldn't work out if it was a cruel or playful delight she was experiencing.

"I assume you are not aware that Ares has been engaged in a centuries long affair with Aphrodite?"

I swallowed hard, a distinctly unpleasant feeling crawling over me, then settling in my stomach like a rock. "Aphrodite? The Goddess of Love?"

"That's the one, yes."

Well, fuck. Fuck, fuck, fuck. I'd seen her twice now, and she was beyond beautiful. Painfully stunning. No wonder Ares didn't want me.

"She's married to Hephaestus, so it's not like they're an actual item or anything, but everyone knows they're at it," Eris continued, pulling the blue thing from the closet and holding it up.

"At it," I repeated dumbly. "So, the Goddess of Love isn't faithful to her husband?"

Eris paused her examination of the garment and

looked at me, eyebrows high. "Sweetie, nobody in Olympus is faithful to their spouses. Except Hades. That delicious specimen of a man is fucking exceptional."

"Right." If the folk around here weren't bothered about being faithful, then hopefully that meant Aphrodite wouldn't smite me into oblivion for kissing her boyfriend. For some reason, I found the idea of upsetting the Goddess of Love a lot more frightening than upsetting the God of War. Go figure.

"Aphrodite has been toying with my little brother for as long as I can remember, and I've never, ever seen him even a little bit interested in anyone else." Another sucker-punch to the gut. Why the hell did I care? *It was just a damned kiss!* "Until you."

My eyes snapped to hers. "Me? What do you mean?"

She gave a tinkling laugh. "Sweetie, if his awkwardness around you wasn't enough, or the way he fought alongside you in the ring, then the man sitting and tended your fucking wounds should be a bit of a clue. Ares does not play well with others, and he is certainly not the nurturing type."

I swallowed down the wave of hope and elation that accompanied her words. Ares had turned me down. He was with Aphrodite. And Eris was *not* to be trusted. No matter how much I couldn't help liking her.

"So you're trying to make me look good to cause friction between Aphrodite and your brother?"

Eris shrugged. "I don't like her, but she creates more disruption than most of the other Olympians put together. She's incredibly fickle, easily bored, dismissive of the rules and more manipulative than I am. Angering Aphrodite is positively a sport for me. The fallout is always worth the effort."

I pursed my lips as I looked at her. "Remind me not to get on the wrong side of you," I said. She grinned at me.

"When Aphrodite realizes you've got the attention of her pet warrior, you'll be begging me to be your best friend."

27

BELLA

"You know, for a woman who hasn't worn a dress in twenty years, you look damn good in one," Eris said, as we both stared at my reflection.

I didn't reply. I couldn't. I was too busy trying to work out how I felt about both what I was looking at, and what I had learned about Ares and Aphrodite.

Eris had made a whole load of alterations to the dress, and she had totally nailed her earlier goal of 'feminine, yet badass'. It was in the Erimosian style, a floaty silk skirt falling almost to the floor, but the band around the waist and hem were decorated with a gold pattern of intertwining swords, rather than the flowers it had before. The top half of the dress had been changed from blue to gold, and was wrapped tightly around my torso like mummy bandages, the gauzy fabric layered up expertly. Little capped sleeves covered my shoulders, in a shape that looked almost like armor. My newly long, wavy hair was pulled back from my face with a blue headband that matched the skirt, with hundreds of tiny gold beads hanging from it.

"Have you deliberately made me look like I'm wearing gold armor?" I asked her. *Armor like Ares,* I left unsaid.

"I've made you look like the Goddess of War," she said. "Do you like it?"

"Yes."

I loved it. There was no point pretending I didn't. I'd spent my whole life trying to understand how my violent, confrontational urges and fierce temper could exist within a person who loved the theater, who loved Disney. And here she was, staring back at me from the mirror. The two halves of me that had never worked together properly, finally, melded. A freaking warrior princess.

I turned to Eris. "Thank you."

"You're welcome," she said with a smile. "Now, I must go and get ready myself. Ares will collect you shortly."

"Wait-" I started, but she gave me a finger wave, and vanished with a flash.

I closed my eyes and took a deep breath. For someone who didn't scare easily, I'd take a freaking acid-breathing Hydra over going to this ball any day of the week.

The knock on my door a half hour later made my heart leap in my chest, and I forced down my trepidation as I stood up. *It was just Ares.* I'd spent the last two days with him. There was nothing to freak out about.

Fire, drums, heat, passion. The flashback to our kiss tore through my mind, and I bared my teeth. *Get a grip, Bella!* I forced myself to picture Aphrodite's beautiful face instead, as I reached the door and pulled it open.

Ares was in full armor and helmet, exactly as I had expected him to be. But I was clearly not dressed as he had expected. A slightly odd noise came from under his helmet, and I saw his eyes widen.

"Just flash us to the party," I snapped, surprising myself with how angry I sounded.

"Your hair..."

"Is longer, yes. Ten fucking points for observation. Get on with it." I could feel my face heating just being in his presence, and I was suddenly desperate not to be alone with him.

"Bella, I-"

"I said let's go, armor-boy!" I cut him off loudly. His eyes hardened, and he straightened.

"Fine." There was a familiar pull in my stomach, a flash, and we were back in the fighting pit.

I blinked around myself, registering the changes from when I'd last been there. The sky above us was no longer bright and clear as it had been during the day. An inky blanket of navy was lit by swirls of glittering clouds corkscrewing over my head, pastel pinks and oranges sparkling in the gloom. The sandy stage had changed too, now dotted with tall marble columns, each with orange flames flickering on top which cast a soft, animated glow over the other folk milling around. Short satyrs and slight young women moved between the guests carrying trays of drinks, and I could hear a harp playing, though could see no musicians. It was beautiful, and unexpectedly calm.

"Bella! I'm so glad you're OK." I turned at Persephone's voice, the Queen hurrying toward me in an exquisite leaf green dress that had a high choker neckline, and black vines embroidered across the edges.

"Oh, yeah, thanks. I heard you came to help."

"Queen Persephone," grunted Ares, then strode away, his armor clanging.

"He's as cheerful as ever then," Persephone said with a smile. "You look amazing! I got a bit of a makeover when I got here as well."

"Thanks, you look awesome too. How do I get one of those drinks?"

Persephone flagged down a satyr and I gulped down most of the drink he handed me in one go. Persephone raised her eyebrows at me. "One of those days, huh?"

"Definitely one of those days."

I chatted to Persephone a while, but I struggled to keep my attention from wandering. Now that my strength was restored, my awareness of the things around me was in full-force, perhaps even more so than usual, and everything was setting me on edge. I didn't know if it was my constant low-level shame and anger about the kiss and resulting rejection, or my trepidation about Aphrodite. Eris had done a good job in setting me up to worry about seeing the Goddess of Love, that was for sure.

"So, the man the demon took, are you two together?" Persephone's words slammed into me, drawing my attention fully back to her. Guilt swamped me.

"No, no, he was my, erm, anger management shrink."

"So no romantic feelings at all? It's just you seemed very upset when you first got here." Her voice was gentle, and not probing. Unlike Eris, who I believed was always trying to get to some information she could use, I got the feeling Persephone actually cared.

"He was the only person who didn't get freaked out by my strength or my temper," I said quietly. "But I guess if he knew what I really was, then that makes sense now. I thought he was my friend."

"Just because he knew you were from Olympus doesn't mean he wasn't your friend."

"His job was to keep an eye on me. He spent eight months trying to convince me that my issues were chemical." I could hear the hurt in my voice as I said the words aloud. "All that time he knew that my temper was part of my soul, my strength part of what made me who I was. Why did he lie? Why not just tell me?"

"I'm sorry," Persephone said softly. "That must be hard."

I shook my head, embarrassed. "No, I'm sorry. I guess I've been avoiding thinking about it much." A little too much, I thought, that damned kiss firing in my memory again. "I have to find him, I'm the only one who knows he was taken. I can worry about our relationship once he's safe."

"Good plan. Things have a way of changing here. Oh, here comes trouble." I glanced to where she was looking over my shoulder, and my heart skipped a beat. The woman walking toward us had raven black hair, alabaster skin and scarlet red lips to match her lace sheath dress. Even though she looked completely different than the last time I'd seen her, I knew at once she was Aphrodite.

"Queen Persephone," she said as she reached us, and her voice was like a caress. She turned to me. "Bella, is it?"

I bowed my head as I answered her. "Yes, that's right."

"You were impressive today."

"Oh," I said. I hadn't expected her to compliment me. "Thanks."

"Have you seen Ares? I need to speak with him."

"No, he went off as soon as we arrived." Relief that she wasn't going to use her divine power to punish me for kissing her lover was washing through me, along with a tiny, unjustifiable glimmer of satisfaction that he hadn't gone straight to her when we got here.

"No matter. I'm sure he'll come to me soon enough," she said. Her eyes moved slowly up and down my dress, and I suddenly felt an overwhelming desire to impress her. I needed her to like me, to love me even. I wanted to be like her, have eyes as deep and mesmerizing, have lips as full and soft, skin as smooth and touchable-

"My, my, you are still mostly human," she said with a small smirk. The feeling broke, and fresh embarrassment pricked at me as I realized she'd been using her power on me.

I had wanted to worship her. Hell, I had wanted to *be* her. The thought of her invading my mind like that, making me want to change who I was, made the nervousness Eris had instilled in me tip dangerously toward anger. I didn't take well to being played with.

"Yes, I am still mostly human," I answered stiffly.

"You really should learn to use the mediocre power you have to guard yourself, little girl," she said quietly.

"Little girl?" I repeated. My hearing had narrowed to just us, and my vision was tightening, red tingeing the edges.

"Yes. You are little, Bella. Do not forget how little you are. I am one of the twelve most powerful beings in the world, and you are tiny. Tiny in size, power and influence. Tiny in the mind of the God of War."

"You're pissed because you know he likes me," I snarled, the red mist descending, and the knowledge that goading a goddess was a seriously bad idea abandoning me completely.

Aphrodite laughed. "Likes you? He worked well with you today because he has no choice. He needs his power back. And I'm the reason he wants it back so badly. I won't fuck him until he's strong again." She whispered the last words as she leaned close to me, a cruel smile distorting her beautiful face.

Every instinct in me wanted to punch her, but my arms seemed to be glued to my sides. Before I could say another word she spoke again. "Whatever it is you think you have with him, forget it. Little Bella in her ugly little war dress will never be able to compete with the Goddess of Love. This is one fight you will lose."

"He's not a fucking prize," I snapped, and her smile widened.

"Oh, but he is. And a fine one at that."

"If you're not going to let me hit you, fuck off," I hissed. Aphrodite chuckled.

"I can see why you might think you two have something in common," she said, straightening and moving back. "You are as impulsive and idiotic as he is."

"I'd rather be impulsive and idiotic than cruel."

"Bella, dear, Ares is all three. You are out of your depth."

Without another word she turned on her heel, striding away across the sand, beaming at everyone she passed. I felt my arms loosen by my side and they sprang up automatically, fists balled. My heart was hammering, fury rolling through my body.

"Woah there," said Persephone, and her voice startled me. Her presence had faded to nothing when Aphrodite had been taunting me.

"How can she talk about him like that? She doesn't fucking love him, she's playing with him!"

Persephone touched my arm, glancing around us as she spoke in a hushed voice. "Bella, the gods can mask conversations from others. Only you two know what you just said to each other, and it sounds like it should probably stay that way."

"Everyone should know how nasty she is!"

"Bella, please, listen to me. Making a scene is not going to end well, I promise you. She's not a goddess you want to go up against."

The anger had eased enough with Aphrodite's departure for me to know Persephone was right, but frustration replaced the fury fast. If Ares and Aphrodite were together, fine. But for her to talk about him like he was just some toy, some shiny trophy? Telling him she would only sleep with him when he had his power back was the same as saying she didn't want him for what he really was, only for his strength. It was cruel. If a man told me he wouldn't sleep with me unless I had bigger boobs or longer hair or a bigger bank balance, I'd tell him to go fuck himself. Why was Ares letting her treat him this way?

I bit down on the inside of my cheek, hard.

Why did I care?

Whatever it was between me and Ares that made the drums bang and the fire dance was physical. Nothing deeper than that. I had no right at all to get involved. He was a grown-ass man, he didn't need his freaking honor or heart defended by me. And if Aphrodite was jealous of us spending time together, or whatever it was that had made her go all mighty-goddess-bitch on me, there was nothing I could do about that.

The knowledge that she could call me names and belittle me, and I couldn't do a thing about that either, bothered me though. Of course it did. She had basically just challenged me to a fight I couldn't win. That was like offering freaking drugs to an addict. But it wasn't a real fight. When you won a fight you earned money, respect, a title. You didn't win a fucking man. That wasn't how it worked.

I glared into the crowd where she had disappeared, trying to let my anger go. I needed to help Ares win the Trials, catch the escaped demon, and save Joshua. Aphrodite's love-life and bad fucking attitude was not my problem.

28

ARES

I could feel Bella's anger as she stared after Aphrodite. Unease was gripping my muscles in a vice-like hold as I watched the Goddess sashay through the crowd.

She knew. I knew that she would sense something if she spoke to me, which was why I had done my best to melt into the shadows since arriving.

But somehow she knew before she even saw my face.

"It's not like you to play so well with others."

The voice belonged to my sister, and my stomach sank. "Eris, not now."

"You know, that lover of yours is going to make Bella's life a misery if you fight so well with her tomorrow."

"I have to work with her," I grunted.

"Not necessarily."

"You're suggesting I work against her now?" I

turned to Eris, scowling. "Earlier today you yelled at me for draining her power."

"That's because you had another fight to complete straight away," she shrugged, her burgundy gown rippling as her shoulders moved. "Tomorrow is the last one. Drain her all you like."

"It's only the last one until the next Lord's Trial," I snapped.

"I'm sure she'll have time to recover before then."

I narrowed my eyes at her, and she sipped from her glass. "I thought you liked Bella," I said. "Why are you telling me to do this? She'll hate me."

"Ares, I don't like anyone, you know that. And what's your problem? You've already done it once. Do you like her?"

Eris' eyes sparkled as she looked into mine.

"I just want my power back."

"You *do* like her," Eris breathed, delight on her face.

"Don't be stupid." My eyes flicked to Aphrodite instinctively, and Eris caught the look and snorted.

"Sweetie, last I checked, you two were not exclusive. You know she's with someone different every night, right? She's the Goddess of Love, for fuck's sake."

Heat and anger burned through my veins at the thought, and I was glad for my helmet hiding my reaction. "Go away, Eris."

"You're always saying that to me," she pouted. "Baby brother, at some point that girl is going to find out just what a monster you really are. May as well get it out in the open now." She gave me a small, knowing smile, and strode off toward the crowd.

I leaned hard against the column beside me, grinding my teeth. What a gods-awful mess.

For centuries I had shared the bed of the most beautiful being in existence. So why, why, why I had I never felt anything like what I had when Bella kissed me? Why had I never seen fire burn in Aphrodite's eyes? Why had the drums of war never beat to the rhythm of my racing pulse when Aphrodite kissed me? *Because whenever I was with Aphrodite, I was only aware of her.* I was never aware of my own feelings or body. I always wanted more of her delight, her pleasure, her satisfaction, only considering my own release later. But with Bella... I'd desired her for my own pleasure, unable to stop myself imagining what it would feel like to be inside her, what her own pleasure would have felt like *for me.*

I let out an angry hiss. This was untenable. Bella could not be more off limits. The memory of the hurt on her face earlier, her anger with me, made that unfamiliar feeling grip my chest again. The one I believed to be guilt.

I couldn't tell her why kissing her was such a bad idea. I couldn't tell her anything, and for the first damned time in my life, I felt guilty.

I tried to rationalize my confused emotions as I watched the party, unwilling to believe they couldn't be explained. I was the God of War, and as such had an innate appreciation for valor and fighting skill. Bella's courage and her fire compelled me to respect her. The thrill of adrenaline I had experienced after fighting the Hydra must have combined with that, resulting in my desire for her. The fact that I could taste my own power within her now just made her feel more connected to me than she actually was.

Yes. That was surely all there was to it.

But she felt it too.

Maybe Eris was right. Maybe the best way to end anything we might accidentally have triggered was for me to do the one thing I knew would make her despise me. Show her what a monster I was. Maybe I should use up all of her power again, in the next fight. It would prove to Aphrodite that I didn't have any allegiance to Bella, and it would ensure Bella would never kiss me again.

The jolt of loss I felt at just thinking about never having my lips so close to hers again only served to strengthen my resolve.

Whatever it was that was causing these feelings had to be stopped.

29

BELLA

I t was easy to spot the Olympian gods amongst the guests. If they didn't stand out so much for their sheer aura of power, the many other guests fawning over them would have identified them as special. Once again, I was disappointed not to see Hera. I was desperate to ask about Zeeva, and her interest in me.

Hermes and Dionysus both came to speak to me though. I liked Hermes instantly, his cheerful red beard and hair brightening my mood as soon as he began to speak. He asked me about being human, and where my power came from. When I told him I didn't know, he shrugged and told me that he couldn't keep track of his offspring either, and that was one of the many troubles of being immortal. He didn't look troubled though, and was soon waving cheerfully at me as he left to talk to a woman who was over ten feet tall.

Dionysus, on the other hand, I struggled to talk to at all because his words were so slurred and his accent so odd so that I couldn't really understand him. In the end a small troupe of silent women with tree-bark skin - just like the girl at the caravanserai - gave me apologetic grins and carried him off.

"Well fought today," said a male voice as I watched Dionysus disappear with mild amusement. I turned to see Pain, smiling at me. He looked positively regal, in a white robe adorned with gold embroidery, and even more bling than before dripping from his neck and fingers. "I look forward to seeing more of the two of you tomorrow."

"Don't suppose you want to give me a heads up? Tell me what to expect?"

He chuckled. "Absolutely not. You look ravishing tonight." His eyes turned darker, and that uneasy feeling I got whenever he was around shuddered across my skin.

"Thanks. I'm going to find Eris," I said, starting to turn around.

"You're not just any demigod," he said quietly. I stopped, and turned back to him slowly.

"I'm mostly human," I said flatly. "You got a problem with my magic, take it up with Ares." At some point I was going to have to talk to the jackass God of War, just to establish what I was and wasn't supposed to tell people. Since Eris had reacted with so much interest when I told her that Ares had called me the Goddess of War, I now felt reluctant to share the information.

To be honest, I felt reluctant to share any information at all with Pain. He freaked me out, and that wasn't that easy to do.

"You're made of the same power we are," he said, his voice low. More discomfort coiled in my belly. He was right. I shared Ares' power, and Ares said he had created the Lords of War. We did share something.

"If that's true, then I'm glad you got the kinky pain fetish, and I just got quick feet and a solid punch," I said. His smile widened.

"We are very, very interested in you, Bella."

"Look buddy, I've had plenty enough interest from crazy deities for one evening. I'm going home, I've got a fight to prepare for." I said the words with over-bluffed confidence. The truth was, I had no freaking idea at all how to get back to the caravanserai. I'd only ever been flashed to the fighting pit, and I couldn't even see the city over the top of the high seats ringing us.

But I did want to leave. My simmering temper had reached its limit of dealing with self-important pricks, and the tension in avoiding Ares was beginning to feel suffocating.

If I had to find my own way back, I would.

"I need to rest also. We will leave now." Ares' deep voice made my stomach lurch, and I didn't know if that was because he'd startled me or for a different reason entirely.

"You know that only myself or one of the twelve Olympians can flash a being into my city," Pain said with a smile. He gestured at Ares. "Please, go ahead." Ares didn't move, and it was too dark for me to see his eyes clearly behind his helmet, but I was willing to bet they were furious. Pain knew he wasn't strong enough to do it. *I* wasn't strong enough for him to use my power to do something only an Olympian could do.

"Flash us back to the caravanserai," Ares ground out.

"As you wish, mighty one," said Pain, his voice sly and cold. "I look forward to tomorrow." He gave me one last lingering look, then with a flash we were outside the grand little tower in the center of Erimos.

"Why didn't you go and ask one of the other gods to flash us back?" I asked immediately. "Why give Pain the satisfaction?"

"Because the more black marks he adds to his list, the more I can punish him when I am divine again," Ares hissed. I raised my eyebrows, but said nothing. "Did you eat?" he asked me abruptly. His question surprised me enough into answering.

"Yeah, that barbecue stuff they were passing around."

"Good. Then I shall retire."

"Right. Good," I said. Why did he care if I'd eaten? He started to walk up the steps to the tower, and I followed after him. "Look, Pain knows I share your power. I don't know what I'm supposed to tell people."

Ares' steps seemed to slow a second, then resumed faster.

"Tell them what you wish."

"What I wish? I don't know anything about my power, you won't tell me!"

"I told you that you are the Goddess of War. That is

all you need to know." He started up the stairs, and I hurried after him.

"But Eris and Persephone both said there is no Goddess of War."

"Your existence says otherwise."

"Will you stop stamping off and look at me! This is important!"

He did stop, glaring at me through the eye slits in his helmet. "It is not remotely important. Until I regain my own power, I can access a shadow of it via you. That is all that is important."

"Did you make me, like the Lords?" I demanded, ignoring the twisting feeling in my gut that his dismissal was causing.

"No," he snapped, then flinched, as though he hadn't meant to answer. "Enough." He turned, resuming his stomp up the stairs even faster.

"You're an asshole," I said, but he didn't stop. "You bring me here, turn my life upside down, use me for my power, and are selfish and callous enough to tell me my own history is unimportant."

He said nothing, just marched on until he was out of my vision. A moment later I heard a door slam. Cold fury trickled down my spine and it wasn't all for him. I was angry with myself. I was a fool to think he cared about me. I was a fool to have kissed him. Worse, I was a fool to want to do it again.

∾

I slammed my own door hard when I was inside my room, just to prove that two could play at the stamping and sulking game. I was so caught up in seething with him that the sight of Zeeva on my bed surprised me enough to elicit a small yelp.

"*Calm down,*" she said inside my head. I glared at her.

"Where the fuck have you been?"

"*Meeting with my mistress,*" the cat answered, blinking slowly. The sight of her did something to my slightly fried brain. Other than my little knife and my Guns N' Roses t-shirt, she was the only truly familiar thing I had in Olympus. I had been pouring my issues into the uninterested ears of my cat for the last eight years, and seeing her there, when my brain was so full of conflicting emotions and useless information, made my mouth move before I could stop it.

"Yeah? Well since I last saw you, I defeated a Hydra, nearly burned my damned arm off, kissed the fucking God of War, got threatened by the Goddess of Love, and attracted the interest of a creepy-as-fuck deity who embodies pain. I could have done with some freaking assistance before now."

Zeeva's tail flicked as I took a deep breath, still glaring. "*You kissed him?*"

I closed my eyes. "Yes. And Aphrodite's crazy, and he's an ass and I just shouldn't have done it," I groaned.

"*No. You probably shouldn't have,*" she said. I opened my eyes and looked at her.

"Zeeva, please. I need more than anyone is giving me. I need to know where I came from, I need to know how to use my power, I need to know if I can trust Ares. Why am I connected to him?" I stopped myself adding, *why can't I stop thinking about him?*

"*That is precisely why I have been with Queen Hera,*" she said. "*I needed her permission to help you. When I saw what Ares did to you in your first fight, I went to her at once.*"

My mouth fell open. "I thought you said you didn't care about me?"

"*What I care about is you surviving these absurd Trials and catching that demon.*"

"Why?"

"*Because that is what my mistress wishes. Now, I can't tell you where you came from. Before you protest, that is because I do not know. I have my suspicions, but they will not help you until I can confirm them.*" I clamped my mouth shut, stopping the protestation she had correctly guessed was coming from escaping. "*I can, however, help you access your power.*"

Excitement exploded inside me. "Seriously?"

"*Yes. Hera and I believe it is important that Ares can't take it all again. If he went too far, he could kill you. And the easiest way to stop that from happening is to teach you to control it yourself. But Bella, you must use it with wisdom and restraint, or you will drain yourself.*"

"Drain myself?"

"*Yes. Lots of demigods who come into their power late get overwhelmed by it. If you were to do that in Pain's test tomorrow, against a foe, draining yourself could be fatal. It would leave you unconscious and Ares powerless. Do you understand me?*"

"Yes. I'm not as impulsive as I seem, I swear." That wasn't entirely true, but her words were hitting home. I had no intention of dying in Pain's fighting pit, power or none. Excited energy was making my palms sweat, and I was rocking back and forth on my slippered heels. "How do I use my magic?"

"Motivation is at the heart of it. Once you know where inside you the well of power is, then needing or wanting something badly enough will activate it."

"How do I find this 'well' of power?"

"Where is your weapon?"

I blinked at her. "You mean my flick-knife?"

"Yes."

I reached into one of the deep pockets in my billowing skirt and pulled out my little knife. "What's this got to do with my power?"

"You are bonded with that weapon. It is small and unassuming, but fast and lethal. It represents you." I looked down at the knife in my palm. I'd never really thought about it like that, but it made sense. *"You have been inadvertently channeling your power into that blade for a long time. It is time to take it back."*

I stared at Zeeva in astonishment. "But the power can't be in my knife. When Ares uses it I can feel it in my stomach. When I'm fighting I feel it in my vision and my hearing and my muscles. It's not in the knife."

"It is true that a certain amount resides within you. But the real power? The divine power? The more human you became, the more had to pass to the blade. Every time you or Ares has accessed your power since you came here, your

blade has been with you. You are the conduit. Now you need to become the source."

I let out a long breath, the hairs on my skin standing on end with excitement as I clutched the blade in my damp hands. Every other crazy thing I'd experienced since leaving that shitty concrete box in London paled to nothing as the knife began to heat in my hands.

"Zeeva, it's doing something," I whispered.

"Yes. Name the blade. Accept it as a part of your soul."

"*Ischyros,*" I breathed, then looked up at Zeeva, alarmed. "What is that word? How do I know it?"

I could hear the smile in the cat's voice as she answered me. *"It is the name of your weapon. It means mighty."*

Heat exploded from the flick-knife, but unlike the searing pain from the inside of the Hydra, this heat was blissful. It spread through my body like an unstoppable force, alighting every nerve ending I had. The knife began to vibrate in my hand, and as the heat moved through my chest and seemed to gather under my ribs, the knife began to shine a bright red. It was growing.

I gaped as my faithful little knife morphed in front of my eyes, transforming into a full-sized sword. I brought my other hand to the hilt, marveling at its weight, and when I drew the blade closer to look at it, the heat inside me suddenly stopped rushing around, as though it had found the place it needed to be.

I knew this sword. I knew the intricate swirling pattern etched up the center of the steel. I knew the two deep dark rubies set into each side of the gold hilt. I knew its weight in my hands as I moved it from palm to palm. I knew it and I loved it. "*Ischyros*," I murmured, and strength flared in my chest.

I looked up at Zeeva. "This is fucking awesome."

"Oh no," said Ares as soon as I opened my door to him the next day. He was wearing his armor but holding his helmet under his arm, so I got the pleasure of seeing his beautiful face fall. I beamed at him, holding my sword up between us.

"Oh yes, armor-boy. I've got a fucking sword."

"How did you-" he began, but I cut him off.

"Let's just get something straight right now. I have no problem with you using my power. But we share."

He glared at me. "I don't even know if that is possible," he said slowly. "And besides, just because you have a sword, doesn't mean you can actually use your power."

"Oh, you mean like this?" I asked cheerily, and pulled on the well of heat now burning steadily under my ribs.

Ischyros grew a foot longer, glowing red.

I wasn't going to admit to him that Zeeva had only taught me how to do that, heal small wounds, and guard my mind against other gods' influence. The last one was the one she said was the most important, and had made me practice the longest before I finally fell asleep.

But glowing swords were way more fun if you asked me.

Ares narrowed his eyes, and I felt a tug in my tummy. He grew a foot taller.

I scowled. I didn't know how to add a foot to my height. In fact, I'd probably have to add four to be taller than him. But Zeeva's warning about using magic wisely rang in my mind. I had a long time to learn more tricks. Right now, I needed to be ready to fight alongside this jackass, not against him.

"See. Easy. I use a bit, you use a bit," I said, schooling my expression into nonchalance.

Ares shrank back down.

"You look different," he said, then instantly looked like he regretted saying it.

"Erm, my hair is still long," I said awkwardly. Plus I was still wearing the jeweled blue headband to keep it back from my face. I really quite liked it. I had also found some proper leather fighting trousers in the closet, along with boots that were nowhere near as comfortable as my own acid-destroyed steel toecaps.

"We should go," Ares said. Our eyes met, and the distant, faded sound of a drum banged somewhere far away.

In a rush, the memory of that kiss filled every crevice of my mind, and I felt heat leap to my cheeks.

He looked down quickly at his helmet, then lifted it clumsily to his head.

"Yes," I said hurriedly. "Let's go."

If it were possible, the crowd lining the bleachers in the fighting pit was even larger and louder than the day before. Ares had flashed us to the middle of the sandy stage, rather than the plush box we had arrived in yesterday, and as I turned in a slow circle, waving at the spectators, there was a flash of red and the three Lords appeared before us.

"You left the party too early last night, mighty one," said Pain ingratiatingly, bowing his head.

"Indeed. Aphrodite put on quite a show once you had gone. It was a shame you had to miss it. She's quite a goddess." Panic's words caused Ares to stiffen, and irrational anger to roil inside me.

"You know, if we get nothing else out of these Trials, Aphrodite's attentions will have made the whole thing worthwhile," said Terror. His voice was hissing and calm and so much more cruel than the other two.

"Start the last fight," barked Ares, and all three Lords inclined their heads with smirks, before they vanished with another red flash.

Pain's voice boomed out over the pit. "Good day, Olympus! Thank you for gathering to watch the mighty Ares, God of War, take on my Trial of pain!"

There was something about the way he said pain that suggested we really wouldn't enjoy what was coming. I shifted my weight restlessly. Whatever it was, it couldn't be as painful as searing the skin off my arm. I had magic and pastes to heal wounds afterward, I reassured myself. This was just about proving we could endure his Trial and I knew I could handle anything that creep might throw at us.

"And he is joined in the pit by the delightful Bella, Goddess of War!" I froze, looking up at the crowd as fevered exclamations broke out everywhere. *I guess it was a good job that wasn't supposed to be a secret*, I thought, the attention making me awkward. Persephone or Eris must have told them who I was after we left the party. Did it matter if these people knew I was a goddess? Did they know I only had a little bit of power? They'd already seen me fight, so they couldn't be expecting magical fireworks.

I took a long breath through my nose, moving *Ischyros* from hand to hand as I let it out through my mouth. Why should I give a shit what these people thought? I didn't feel like the damned Goddess of War, I was just Bella, except now I had a magic sword.

"And now, to fight! Disable the hundred-hander to win!"

"Hundred-hander? For the love of sweet fuck, tell me there isn't something that has a hundred hands," I said, looking at Ares.

"Of course they have a hundred hands, why else would they be called that?" he snapped back. "They are ancient Titans, and exceptionally strong."

"Fantastic," I replied through gritted teeth. The sound of rushing water reached my ears, and my eyes darted around as the red mist descended. My sword hummed in my hand and I gripped it tighter. A delicious sense of confidence and strength surged through my body, my focus sharpening and muscles alert and tense.

I was born to do this.

With an unearthly roar, a column of water burst from the center of the pit, shooting fifty feet into the air like a geyser, before vanishing as abruptly as it had appeared. But left in its wake was one of the strangest creatures I had ever seen.

Even larger than the Hydra, the thing must have been between twenty and thirty feet tall, easily the size of a house. Its skin looked rubbery and scarred, and was a weird mix of deep and pale blues. Its eyes were deep-set and dark, and the overly large mouth under its squashed nose was filled with brown and broken teeth. But those details kind of paled into insignificance as I stared up at its torso.

The thing was *covered* in arms. They were everywhere. They came out of every available bit of skin on the creature's chest, ribs, shoulders, back, all the way down to its hips. I could easily believe that there were a hundred of them, each ending in a gnarled, clawed five-fingered hand.

"Cottus," roared Ares, and I looked at him in alarm.

"Is that its name?" I hissed.

"A pleasure to meet you, young lady," the hundred-hander boomed and I looked back to it in shock. "And I'm a 'he', not an 'it'."

"I, erm, sorry. Hi," I stammered.

"It will be a shame to kill you today. I like your hair. But you, little God..." All of his hands pointed suddenly at Ares. "I will be very pleased indeed to kill you today."

Laughter rippled through the crowd, and I looked between Cottus and Ares. "I'm guessing you two have history?"

"We do," he growled.

There was a little shimmer around the Titan giant, and the next thing I knew, many of his ugly hands were holding bows, and small arrows were clutched in others.

"Your Lord of War has provided me with some most interesting weapons," Cottus grinned, and something slimy dripped from the corner of his mouth. I tried to keep from showing how much he grossed me out, concentrating instead on one of the arrows. I couldn't see them clearly enough to glean anything though.

With a sudden jerk, about twenty of his arms moved, and with lightning speed at least ten bows were drawn, arrows pointing straight at us.

The crowd sucked in a huge collective breath and Cottus spoke again. "Time to die, God of War."

No magic sword was going to stop that many arrows, I realized, my stomach lurching. We were in serious trouble.

The wave of arrows soared toward us, and I felt a sharp pull in my gut and watched in muted amazement as they all burst into flame, falling harmlessly as ash to the ground.

"I can't do that many more times," Ares shouted, urgency in his voice as he began to run toward Cottus. "You're not strong enough."

I couldn't help the indignant flash that came with the words, 'you're not strong enough', but I held my tongue as I raced after him. My legs felt stronger and faster as I moved, *Ischyros* hot in my hands.

I was pretty certain that the hundred-hander's arrows would reach the edges of the fighting ring, and he had damned arms all the way around his body. There was no place that would be out of range of the bows except one.

Directly underneath him.

Ares must have come to the same realization because he was pelting forward, racing to reach the giant's feet, his powerful legs moving him faster than me.

But Cottus had already drawn the bows back again and shifted his arms, half of them now pointing at me, the others straight down at Ares.

A rain of arrows flew through the air, and my stomach twisted with the inevitable realization that I couldn't stop them.

They must have reached Ares a split-second before me, because his shout of pain preceded the first sharp piercing of my arm. I felt arrows bounce off my leather corset, both on my body and the wide shoulder straps, but at least two met skin.

And thank fuck it was only two. These were not

normal arrows. The one that had punctured my left arm felt as though it was made of fire, and it was pouring flames into my body, searing heat flashing under my skin. The one that had hit my thigh had only just got through the leather, but it was enough to feel like my whole freaking leg was freezing solid, the icy pain so intense that I could hardly breathe.

As the pain in my leg and arm began to overwhelm me and my pounding run started to falter, I felt a pull in my stomach. As Ares' shouts fell silent I remembered with a jolt that I could use magic.

I drew on the well of power under my ribs, trying to make it focus on the agony in my body. A soothing heat leaped to life in my center, spreading out fast, and I felt my strength and speed returning as the white-hot pain lessened ever-so slightly.

I nearly collided with Ares as I reached Cottus' feet, and the giant stamped and roared. We had seconds before he moved, and my usually impeccable judgment of my opponent's next move was clouded by the pulsing waves of fire and ice burning through my nerve endings. I reached down to where I knew the arrow had hit my thigh, but there was nothing there.

"The arrows are absorbed into your body," panted Ares, as we both skipped to the side, staying under Cottus as he danced around, trying to expose us.

"You can't defeat me from under there!" the giant laughed.

I got a stark visual of when I'd seen men in the ring go for the one area that was always out of bounds, and raised an eyebrow at Ares.

"Can we get him in the nuts?" I asked. We both looked up at the fabric-clad genitalia of the giant above us, and I swallowed a wave of revulsion and unease. Besides being gross, it wasn't really a sporting thing to do. But he *was* trying to kill us.

Before either of us could say another word, Ares jumped at the tree-trunk-like leg of the giant. It was twice his height, and Cottus lifted his huge limb and shook it as Ares pulled himself up the rubbery flesh, reaching the bottom of Cottus' shorts easily. Another wave of pain moved through my body and spurred me into action. I threw myself at the giant's other leg and started climbing.

"Get off!" the giant bellowed, shaking and stamping both legs in turn. I clung on to anything I could get a grip on, trying to ignore how weird his skin felt. Once I reached his shorts it was easier, the fabric offering more handholds.

A hand swiped at me, and I only just ducked my head out of the way of it in time. I was in reach of his lower arms now. An arrow whizzed past my ear and I scrambled round, trying to get to the inside of his thigh and move lower, back out of reach of his freaky arms.

I felt a tug in my stomach and tipped my head back, trying to see Ares.

I knew at once something was wrong.

He was a few feet higher than me, on the front of Cottus's thigh. Arrows were pinging off his armor, but a few must have been getting through because his body was flinching repeatedly. But I was focused on his eyes through the slits in his helmet. They were fixed on mine, and even from this distance, I could see that there was something wrong.

The pull in my stomach turned into a wrench, and Ares began to glow gold, moving so suddenly and so fast that he became a blur again. My vision wobbled.

The traitorous lying, evil fucking bastard was going to use all my power again.

Fury filled me instantly, hotter and harder than the waves of pain the arrows had left behind. The heat under my ribs exploded in a flash, and I yanked back on the invisible cord in my stomach as hard as I possibly could with a scream.

Ares fell. The gold blur whizzed past me, slamming into the ground with a grunt and a metallic clank. But I barely noticed. Because I was fucking glowing.

I stared at my arms, still clinging to Cottus' shorts. They were glowing gold. Cottus raised his leg again, but it was like we were underwater, and he was moving in slow motion. I saw an arm reach down toward me, ready to take a swipe, but it would take an age to reach me, he was moving so slowly.

Seizing my chance, I launched myself up, the strength in my arms and legs, and the speed with which I found myself pulling my body higher astonishing me. When I reached Cottus' waist I began pulling myself up his arms like I was a monkey climbing a tree, leaping from one slow-moving arm to the other like I'd been doing it my whole life. By the time I reached his neck, I was radiating gold light, and I saw the giant's pupil contract, and his eyes widen in blissfully slow detail.

The Titan giant had underestimated me, and now he was paying the price.

I leaped up onto his enormous shoulders, grabbed hold of an ear the size of my head and yanked *Ischyros* from its loop on my belt. Holding the tip of the blade an inch from Cottus' left eye, I spoke.

"Submit."

The world around me sped up again, and I heard the crowd fall utterly silent as they took in the scene before them. Cottus took a heavy breath, his huge eye trained on me.

"You win this one, little lady," he said, then vanished in a flash of green as a gong sounded.

BELLA

I pulled hard on the heat inside me as I fell through the air, willing anything to break my fall. I let out a gasp of relief as I hit a cushion of soft air, and then rolled off it, landing on the sandy ground.

"How did you do that?" growled Ares' voice, but I barely heard him over the roar of the crowd and the blood pounding in my ears. I launched myself to my feet, whirling to face him.

"You asshole!" I screamed at him, rage like I had never experienced filling me. I was glowing again, bright and fierce, and I was holding *Ischyros* at Ares' chest. "I trusted you, and you were going to do it again! You were going to leave me empty and broken!" I was furious. And I knew, deep-down, that the betrayal was worse because of whatever we shared. Telling myself over and over that nothing could happen between us had not changed the longing in my core, the belief that something was meant to exist between us.

But his actions had shattered everything.

"It was the quickest way to win the fight and get it over with," Ares said, only just loudly enough for me to hear him. "You would have recovered."

"No! I don't give a shit about your excuses, you know how it feels to be stripped of your power! You know!" I could feel hot tears of rage and frustration welling behind my eyes, burning. Please gods, don't let me fucking cry in front of him. I drew harder on the rage, and my skin glowed brighter.

"I didn't know you had the power to defeat him yourself. I didn't know you were this strong. How were you hiding it from me?"

"Hiding it from you? Are you fucking serious? You don't get to accuse me of anything, you lying bastard!"

Fire was dancing in his eyes, but there were no drums. And rather than call to me, I felt nothing but the need to douse the flames.

"I made a strategic decision."

"I fucking hate you." The words were out of my mouth before I could stop them, and I loathed how much they made me sound like a petulant teenager. Or a betrayed lover. "I will never, ever share my magic with you. You don't deserve a fucking drop of power, you selfish, arrogant-" My tirade was cut off as the Lords of War flashed into existence around us, Terror clapping his marble hands together slowly.

Pain's voice boomed through the pit. "Ares and Bella win the first Trial! We'll find out what my esteemed brother, Panic, has in store for them shortly." The crowd continued to roar and cheer, but I couldn't take my eyes off Ares. How could he? After fighting alongside me, nursing me, fucking *kissing* me, I genuinely hadn't believed he would leave me unconscious and drained in the ring a second time.

"Shall we continue this elsewhere?" said Terror silkily. "Much as Olympus loves a bit of drama, we should keep some things to ourselves."

Yet more light flashed around us and we were all in the box at the top of the pit.

"Stop fucking doing that!" I yelled, rounding on Pain. "I'm sick to death of being flashed all over the place without anyone telling me!"

"It looks like you'll be able to do it yourself soon," Pain answered with a smile. "You're a fast learner."

"And you're as much of an asshole as him. Send me back to the caravanserai, now."

I needed to be somewhere I could let off this rage, immediately. My temperature was at fever pitch, my blood feeling like it was actually boiling. One more minute in the company of these dishonest maniacs, and I would lose my shit completely. And now that I was glowing and had a big fucking sword, that seemed like a seriously bad idea.

"Do you not want to see your friend before you go?" asked Terror.

I froze. "What?"

"Well you've done so well already," he said smoothly. "We feel you deserve a reward."

Alarm bells rang in my head as I stared at his stone face, the black swirling across it. There was no way these men wanted to help or reward me.

"We've decided that as you weren't the one challenged to the Trials in the first place, you should be given the chance to catch the demon yourself. You don't need to compete."

They were trying to separate me and Ares. They knew he would lose if he didn't have me.

I looked at the God of War. He stared back at me from under his helmet, and I couldn't identify the emotion churning in his eyes.

And I didn't care.

"How?" I demanded, turning back to the Lords. Terror waved his hand, and a large circular part of the air between us shimmered and rippled. As I stared, the rippling cleared, and the room full of stone beds came into focus. The beds were all empty, but I was sure it was the same room.

"Just step though. If you catch or kill the demon yourself, I suppose Ares can't complete Oceanus' quest and won't get his power back. But you'll be able to save your friend before something happens to him."

My heart was galloping in my chest, a million emotions crashing into each other in my head. I looked back to Ares. If I stepped through that portal I was basically signing his death warrant.

But hadn't he just been willing to do the same? To leave my life to chance? He might survive the Trials without power. He wasn't exactly weak. I looked through the portal. I could see blood, dried onto the stone beds, and a vision of Joshua with his glassy dead eyes and bleeding chest filled my mind.

If I had the chance to save him now, I had to take it.

I opened my mouth, the impulse to tell Ares I was

sorry rising in me fast. But as I looked at him, the rage swelled again. He had tried to drain me. Again. After swearing not to. He cared nothing for me.

And I owed him nothing.

Gripping *Ischyros* tightly in my hand, I stepped through the portal.

THANKS FOR READING!

Thank you so much for reading The Warrior God, I hope you enjoyed it! If so I would be very grateful for a review! They help so much; just click here and leave a couple words, and you'll make my day :)

You can order the next book, The Savage God, here.

You can also get exclusive first looks at artwork and story ideas, plus free short stories and audiobooks if you sign up to my newsletter at elizaraine.com.

CPSIA information can be obtained
at www.ICGtesting.com
Printed in the USA
LVHW090019240721
693518LV00003B/54